HER UNEXPECTED ROOMMATE

CIDER BAR SISTERS, BOOK 5

JACKIE LAU

First edition: August 2022
ISBN: 978-1-989610-28-2

Editor: Latoya C. Smith, LCS Literary Services

Cover Design: Flirtation Designs

Cover photograph: Adobe Stock

AUTHOR'S NOTE

Content notes (for the author's note and the rest of the book):
mental illness, suicide

Back when my mom was healthy, I remember she looked forward to turning fifty. She said the whole year was going to be a celebration.

Alas, that's not what happened.

When I was twenty-five and my mother was fifty, I lost her to suicide.

My mother had an episode of severe depression about once every ten years. I, too, was no stranger to depression, and not just because I'd seen her struggle with it. I believe I first became depressed when I was fifteen, and I have never not struggled with mental illness as an adult.

The feeling of being suicidal was something I understood… intimately. And I do think the way I processed that loss had a lot to do with my own experience with depression.

I have long wanted to write a heroine with a similar experience to me, who'd also lost a parent to suicide and dealt with treatment-resistant depression herself. It was part of Rose's story from the time I planned out the Cider Bar Sisters series early in 2020, but I didn't feel ready to write it yet, so I decided hers would be the last book. By the time I began writing the book, late in 2021, I was as ready as I could be.

I don't think this book is too depressing, and I assure you it has a happy ending, but it didn't feel right to call it a rom-com, so this book is categorized a little differently from the other books in the series. Rose lost her mother about ten years before the start of the book, and it's not described in graphic detail, but it's still part of her story.

Rose has compassion for her mother's experiences with depression, but their relationship was complicated by the fact that her mother didn't really "believe" in mental illness even though she was clearly suffering from it herself. When Rose started having problems as a teenager, her mother wasn't supportive, although she was supportive in other areas of Rose's life.

My own relationship with my mother wasn't exactly like Rose's relationship with her mom, but there were some similarities.

I started writing in 2010, several months before my mother's death. The last time I saw her, one of the things I told her was that I'd started writing a novel, and she was happy for me because she knew it was something I'd always wanted to do.

That novel never saw the light of day, but I've now written many, many other books, including *Her Unexpected Roommate*, the final story in the Cider Bar Sisters series.

Jackie Lau

[1]

Rose Pang positioned Fred the Alpaca so it looked like he was drinking the brown sugar boba, which she'd bought at her favorite bubble tea shop on Bloor. He wasn't very steady on his feet, however, and he faceplanted onto the coffee table.

She repositioned the plushie, and once Fred was stable, she snapped a few pictures with her phone. Then she shook up her drink and sipped it as she uploaded the best photo to Instagram. Her alpaca had an Instagram account to showcase his adventures. With his light purple fluff and ever-present smile, he was very photogenic.

Someone else immediately commented on the picture. One of Fred's online plushie friends.

Will you share with me? Penguin Pip asked.

Rose typed a reply, then put down her phone and leaned back on the couch. She snuggled Fred while she finished her boba. Mmm. The caramelized brown sugar was the best.

This wasn't what she'd thought life would be like at thirty-four. Spending Saturday afternoons alone with her favorite plushie and talking to a penguin on Instagram? When she was in university, she'd imagined she'd have a husband and a couple of kids by now. Her view of the future had been hazy, but she'd had one nonetheless.

Her phone rang, and she smiled as she picked it up. "Hi, Dad."

"Rose." It wasn't a video call, but she saw his smile, his thinning white hair, and his wireframe glasses in her mind. "How are you today? Is Sierra back from the cabin?"

"I'm okay," Rose said. "Sierra won't be back until tonight." Her roommate was up north with her boyfriend.

They spoke for a few minutes, and then her father dropped a bit of a bombshell.

"I'm retiring," he said.

"For real this time?"

He chuckled. "Yes, I already gave notice."

"They're going to throw you an awkward party and get one of those ugly cakes you hate."

"Trust me, I know what I'm getting into."

She'd been telling her father for years that he should retire—he was seventy—but now that it was actually happening, it caused a twinge of uneasiness. Made her think of her dad's mortality.

"Are you okay?" she asked. "Like, you're not doing this because you're sick and you haven't told me?"

"Rose," he said, "don't worry about me."

"You know I can't help it."

"I know. But I'm fine. I would tell you if there was something wrong, I promise. I'll have more time to help out when the twins come."

"Tracey's having *twins*?"

"Lou didn't tell you?"

Perhaps Rose would have heard earlier if she lived in Ottawa with the rest of her family—her dad and her two brothers. But she'd moved to Toronto several years ago, and most of the time, she was content here.

"I'll let you go," Dad said several minutes later. "I'm sure you have something exciting planned since it's Saturday night."

Ha.

Part of the problem was that all of Rose's friends were coupled up now. She still saw them somewhat regularly—it wasn't like they'd forgotten about her. But she'd been finding herself alone on weekends a little more often lately, as her friends went on dates and did couple-y things.

Truth be told, she was envious. She wanted to be part of a couple, too.

Of course, being in a relationship wouldn't solve all her problems, but she still liked the idea of it. Someone to cuddle when she watched movies. Someone to take care of her—and the reverse—just a little.

She tried not to want it *too* much; she didn't wish to appear desperate.

But she couldn't help being a bit of a romantic.

Yet she hadn't had a boyfriend in ten years, not since before her mom died, and sometimes, it felt hopeless.

What's wrong with me?

Rose's brain immediately supplied many answers to that question, but she did her best to cut it off. She wouldn't allow herself to go down that path today.

No, she needed to go out. Distract herself. Her friends were busy, but she could have a fun time on her own, right?

Once she'd made a plan for the evening, she went to her bedroom and debated what to wear. She settled on a red sundress that she'd bought last month from an online plus-sized retailer. She'd been waiting for a special occasion to wear it, but why couldn't she wear it just for herself?

Her brain tried to pull her back under, telling her this was pathetic, but she ignored it as she applied her makeup and picked out her shoes.

She was going to have a good time!

She selected some wedge sandals. Since she was going to places that weren't far from the house she shared with Sierra in the Annex, she didn't need shoes that were comfortable for a long walk.

Her first stop was a Japanese restaurant with the best bento boxes. Why did food in rectangular compartments please her so much? She wasn't sure, but she'd always been fond of such things. She ordered the deluxe beef teriyaki bento box and read a book as she waited for the food to arrive. Maybe it didn't look cool to be out alone reading, but whatever. Rose had never been particularly cool.

Next, she headed to Nautilus, a steampunk bar located in a sprawling Victorian house. She'd been here with her friends once before, but she'd always meant to go back. Sometimes exploring a place like this was better when you were alone. You could spend exactly as much time on everything as you wanted and take as many pictures as you desired.

And there were lots of things that deserved a photo. The attention to detail in Nautilus was incredible, especially in the murals, and every room was unique. One had numerous hot air balloons; another had a blimp. Still another had a kraken attacking a ship. In each of the larger rooms, there was a bar, and one of them looked like an old-school science lab, the bartender wearing a white lab coat.

It was early, so it wasn't too busy yet. Rose walked around and snapped pictures upstairs before returning to the first floor. To her delight, there was a table in the basket under the blimp, and it was unoccupied. She rushed to claim it before going to the nearest bar—there was no table service here—and ordering a drink, which came in a glass with gears on the side.

Clasping the drink in her hand, she looked around at the groups of people talking and laughing together, and suddenly, she was hit with an aching loneliness. Negative thoughts crowded her brain again, but she imagined putting them in a box and throwing them into the sea, where they could be eaten by a kraken.

Rose was determined to have a fun night before she went home and snuggled her plushies.

~

Cal Dempsey whistled as he ambled from the subway station to the bar. He was supposed to be meeting Marv's girlfriend tonight, and Marv had chosen this place called Nautilus. Cal had never heard of it before and had no idea what a nautilus was, but that was cool. There would be beer and presumably TVs so he could watch the Jays game as he waited.

Hanging out with Marv sometimes involved waiting. He was often late—and not just ten or fifteen minutes late. Cal had no idea why his friend was like that, but whatever, no big deal. He didn't mind chilling in a bar alone.

He held the door open for a group of women before entering. This place had some kind of old-timey theme, which he didn't really understand, and there were, unfortunately, no TVs. Oh, well. He'd grab a beer, find a seat, and let Marv know he was here. Maybe order some wings.

He sauntered over to the bar and studied the options. Nothing familiar, so he ordered the Captain Nemo Pilsner from the bartender, who wore a strange hat with goggles. Huh.

Cal took a seat at the table beneath a blimp, thinking that looked kinda neat. Someone had forgotten a black sweater on the table—he'd turn it in at the bar when he got his next drink. Perhaps they had some kind of lost and found like at school.

He'd been very familiar with the lost and found at his elementary school. He'd frequently lost his things, which hadn't pleased his parents. They'd written his name in permanent marker on the tags of everything he owned, and he'd usually gotten it back, but not always.

"Hey. That's my seat."

Cal spilled a little beer as he whipped his head around. The woman standing by his table had one hand on her hip and a frown on her face.

He smiled.

"What's so funny?" she demanded.

He'd smiled because she was cute, that was all. A round Asian woman in a red dress, which showed off her body to good effect. Her black hair—a little shorter than his own hair—was tied in a loose bun. Her glasses were squarish, and he'd always liked women with glasses. He had no idea why, but he did.

"That's my cardigan," she said, gesturing at the black sweater on the table.

"I thought someone had forgotten it."

He started to get up. If she was so keen on having this table, she could have it. Wasn't like there were no other tables in the room.

Except Marv might not arrive for a while, and there weren't any games to watch.

And Cal kinda wanted to stay here with her.

"We could share?" he suggested.

[2]

"Uh…share?" Rose's hand tightened on her drink.

"Yeah," the man said. "Unless you're waiting for someone."

He was reclined casually in the small booth under the blimp. A big white guy with long, light brown hair, which was tied back.

She'd always had a thing for long hair on men.

He looked like he didn't have a care in the world as he sipped his beer. His lips curved easily into a smile.

She didn't understand why he'd want to share. He should recognize that she had claimed this table and slink off to another one, dammit! How else was a single person supposed to hold a table while getting a drink? It wasn't like she would have left her purse.

Then the fight went out of her.

She'd spent most of the day giving herself a pep talk, and it was exhausting. This table was rightfully hers, but she didn't want to argue.

She sighed. "It's okay. I'll go."

"Wait." He reached out, then seemed to think better of it. "You're right. It's your table. But I'll keep you company and buy you a drink, if you're interested."

"I already have a drink."

As soon as the words left her mouth, she realized what was happening.

He was hitting on her!

It had been a little while since that had happened. And this guy was super attractive and a bit younger than her.

She eyed him suspiciously.

He started to get up. "There's another table in the corner. I'll—"

"No, no. You can, uh, stay."

She wasn't very smooth, but he just smiled and sat back down. She took the seat across from him. It was a bit cramped in the booth, especially since he was a large, sturdy guy. She couldn't tell how tall he was, but his knees knocked against hers. He was wearing a Jays T-shirt, his biceps bulging underneath it. She bet he had nice muscles elsewhere, too, and he seemed to have a good amount of cushion as well.

When she looked back up at his face, he winked, and her skin heated.

He must have noticed her staring, but he didn't say anything about it. No, it was just that wink, and she swallowed, her throat suddenly dry.

"What's your name?" he asked.

"Rose."

"I'm Cal. You been here before?"

"Yeah," she said. "It's a neat place, isn't it? I love that there's a steampunk bar like this in Toronto."

"Steampunk?"

"You know, like science fiction inspired by the Victorian era."

"Huh. Never heard of it. Coming here was my friend's idea."

She felt a moment of disappointment. He'd head off once his friend arrived.

But then his gaze lazily trailed over her, and her throat was even more parched. He shot her a crooked grin, as though he knew exactly how he was affecting her, and she shifted in her seat.

"What's a nautilus?" he asked. "Some kind of steampunk thing?"

"A type of sea creature, I believe?" It was hard to think clearly right now. "It's also the name of the submarine in *Twenty Thousand Leagues Under the Sea*."

He didn't seem familiar with the novel, but he shot her a grin once more.

Damn, that look should be illegal.

She turned away to steady herself. Though it was fairly cool for a summer day, it felt almost uncomfortably hot in here. As a distraction, she examined the nearby mural and imagined taking a picture of Fred with it. "I wish I'd brought my stuffed alpaca."

Oh, God. She gave her head a shake.

Why was she saying such things? Why was she being so damn *awkward*?

She wasn't usually so awkward, but then again, she wasn't usually talking to a strange guy at a bar. Her friend Nicole made it look easy, but it wasn't. Far from it.

"He has his own Instagram account," Rose said. She'd already mentioned her stuffed alpaca, so how much worse could it get? "I could have taken a picture of him with, I don't know, a little hot air balloon or a kraken. Maybe they have a small aviator hat with goggles somewhere."

Okay, she'd been wrong. It was definitely getting worse, and she could see no way to salvage this conversation.

She stood up. "I'll get going and investigate the rest of the bar. You can have the blimp to yourself and—"

"Rose." He lightly touched her wrist, and she whipped her head back around to look at him. "I'd like if you stayed."

"Uh..."

"I mean, you don't have to. But if you're leaving because you're embarrassed for some reason, there's no need."

He folded his arms behind his head. She didn't know if he was aware of how good his muscles looked like that—was he intentionally showing them off?

Probably.

But that was okay with her. She'd always had a thing for arms; she didn't care about abs. No, arms were where it was at, and his were particularly nice.

"Do you like me?" she blurted out, taking a seat once more. She still felt the warmth of his fingers on her wrist.

"Yes, Rose, I like you."

She refrained from asking why. Though she knew she had many good qualities, she didn't think they'd been on display in the last five minutes.

"You're amusing," he said, answering the question she hadn't asked. He didn't say it in a patronizing way. "And pretty."

She sipped her drink to hide her blush. "What do you do for a living?" There. That was a normal topic of conversation, wasn't it?

"I work for a landscaping company," he said. "You?"

"I'm an electrical engineer."

He whistled, looking impressed. "No wonder you knew what a nautilus was."

"They don't have any relation to each other."

"Po-tay-to, po-tah-to." The corner of his mouth quirked up, as if he knew he was being goofy. Like she'd been, when she'd mentioned Fred the Alpaca out of nowhere.

Rose found herself smiling back.

"Why don't we check out the patio?" she said, speaking without thinking once more.

But this time, upon reflection, she didn't regret her words. It was rather hot and stuffy in here, and this place was supposed to have a nice patio.

"Sure," he said.

After stuffing her cardigan into her purse, she bounced out of her seat, a few drops of her drink splashing over the edge of the glass, and instinctively reached for him with her other hand. He'd enfolded her hand in his before she realized what was happening.

Whoa.

They were holding hands.

She enjoyed his large hand around hers as she skipped out to the patio, feeling slightly giddy—and she didn't think it had anything to do with the booze. She hadn't drunk much, after all.

At the edge of the large patio, there was a tentacle trellis of sorts, which sported many pink roses. The sun had set, but there was ample lighting out here. Many of the lights looked like old gas lamps. She scanned the area for a table—it was getting busy.

"What about there?" Cal pointed to a wrought-iron swinging bench at the far end of the patio.

The words had barely left his mouth before she was scampering toward the bench. Unfortunately, she'd forgotten that she was wearing heels, and she fell onto the flagstone, somehow managing to hold her drink aloft.

"You okay?" he asked, helping her up.

She nodded before taking off again, at a slightly more practical pace. Nobody was going to get there before her. Nobody. The swinging bench seemed romantic, and it was in the shadows, so no one would notice if…

What do you think is going to happen, Rose?

She slid onto the bench, laughing, and put her drink on the table beside it.

"Wow," he said, taking a seat next to her, "when you know where you want to sit, you really are serious about it. First the blimp…"

She glared at him, and he laughed at her faux outrage. She wasn't angry about that anymore. No, instead, she was very aware of his thigh pressing against hers. He had nice thick thighs.

She was also aware of her bare knee touching his—he was wearing shorts, and the skirt of her dress had ridden up. Although there was nothing particularly sexy about knees, there was something about his skin against hers that made her breath catch.

She turned to look at him and nearly startled. For some silly reason, she hadn't been prepared for his face to be that close. He had a neatly trimmed beard, and she couldn't decide whether she was more fascinated by his beard or his mouth.

"I'd happily bring you drinks all night," he murmured, "so you wouldn't need to save your seat with a sweater."

"Yeah?" she said rather breathlessly.

"Mm-hmm. And I think me taking pictures of you under a hot air balloon would be cuter than pictures of your alpaca."

"Fred is very cute." She tried to muster some defensiveness for her alpaca friend, but it was difficult when she was sitting right next to Cal.

His lips curved into that crooked smile once more. "I'm sure he is, but not like you." He curled his arm around her, and the end of his ponytail tickled her neck.

Desire coursed through her body. She wanted to untie his hair and stroke it. Wanted to feel those big hands on her body. And when she looked at his fingers, curled around the chain of the swing, she thought of having one inside her, and she nearly moaned.

He inclined his head in the direction of one of the servers, who was wearing a black corset. "Maybe you could wear one of those."

"You think I'd look good in a corset?"

"I do." When his brown eyes searched hers, she really did forget to breathe for a moment. There were so many things she wanted right now, and he seemed to want what she did. Unlike usual, she didn't overthink it; she let her body guide her.

And when he dropped his head, she tilted hers upward.

~

Tonight wasn't what Cal had expected when he'd left his basement apartment a couple of hours ago. He'd expected a little baseball and beer before his friend showed up, but Marv still hadn't texted. If it were anyone but Marv, Cal might be worried, but he wasn't worrying now.

No, instead he was very, very close to kissing a pretty woman in the garden.

When she puckered her lips, he wrapped one arm around her, pulled her even closer, and kissed her.

He certainly hadn't expected *her* when he'd shown up at this steampunk bar, or whatever it was. But Cal was good at going with the flow, and she was a pretty great way to flow. Her mind kept leaping from one thing to another, and he didn't always keep up, especially when he was distracted by her breasts, which were now pressed against him.

Her mouth was sweet and eager, and when he dipped his tongue between her lips, she released a sigh that went right to his cock and filled his head with various images.

Rose shuddering as he licked her clit.

Rose riding him.

Rose underneath him.

Okay, he wasn't very creative. All the images involved her naked. Though she didn't even have to be naked. He wanted to see her naked, of course, but he could also flip up the bottom of her skirt...

Her sigh turned into a giggle. "I can't believe I kissed someone I barely know."

"Not something you do often?" he asked.

"No. And we're in public! Do you think anyone noticed?" She gestured toward the tables on the patio.

"I dunno. Probably not. But we can find somewhere a little more private."

Her eyes widened, as though this was a shocking suggestion, and he was just about to take it back when she said, "Okay!" and hopped up from the bench.

Damn, she seemed excited, and his cock hardened further.

The bar was in a big old house, with various sections sticking out. Lots of corners. Around the back, they found a hidden area behind a tree, and he lifted her up and pressed her against the brick wall. She squeaked in surprise.

"How's this?" he asked with a smile. He found her reactions to everything so freaking delightful. "Private enough for you?"

She nodded.

He could hear traffic, as well as chatter on the patio. They were definitely still in public, but nowhere near as easy to spot as before.

He kissed her again as he held her against the wall, his hands under her ass. Though the fabric of her dress was thin, it was still too thick for his liking.

One of her hands came up to cup his cheek, and she groaned against his lips. Her touch was tender, but her kisses were needy, like she couldn't get enough of him. He ground his hips against her.

"Oh!" she cried upon feeling his erection.

Yeah, this was going to be a very good night.

He set her down on her feet. Her glasses were no longer straight, so he fixed those before slipping down the neckline of her dress along with one cup of her bra, baring her breast to the night air. As he sucked on her nipple, her hand gripped his hair, urging him on.

When she'd gotten pissed at him for stealing her table, he'd certainly never imagined she'd be like *this*.

He slipped one hand under her dress and ran it along the edge of her panties. "What do you think? Should I try to get you off here?"

"You want to...oh!"

She seemed rather innocent, even if he figured she was about his age.

"Yeah," he said. "I wanna finger you and feel how wet you are for me. You into that?"

She nodded eagerly once more.

He pushed aside the crotch of her panties and slid his fingers through her wetness. Her moisture dripped down his fingers. And her breast was still bare, the nipple a tight peak.

This woman would be the end of him.

Cal bent to suck it again, and she made some strangled noises, followed by whispering his name as her pussy clenched around his finger. He added a second finger and thrust them in and out of her channel, while continuing to pay attention to her breast. He wasn't usually much of a multi-tasker. But this sort of thing? Hell, yes.

When he circled his thumb over her clit, she arched against him.

"Good?" he asked.

Another nod.

Damn, he really did want to get her naked in his bed, but he wanted to make her come here first. Give her a little taste of what he could do.

He lifted his head to kiss her sweet mouth. Her tongue plunged between his lips, catching him off guard, but he sure wasn't complaining. One of her hands dipped to grasp his cock through his shorts, and he gritted his teeth before he returned to kissing her.

Christ, she was even wetter now, and he could smell her arousal. He wanted to bury his face between her legs right here, but he had a feeling that would be a step too far for Rose.

He pushed his fingers a little deeper. "You like that, baby?"

"Yes." It sounded like a struggle for her to get out that single word, and he couldn't help feeling pleased.

"Are you going to…"

He trailed off because she was already trembling in his arms and making soft noises of pleasure. It was the prettiest fucking thing ever.

"Want to come home with me?" he asked.

[3]

Rose couldn't believe it. Less than an hour after meeting Cal, she'd orgasmed on his hand. In public.

Now that she was coming down from that high, she became aware of their surroundings. There were people on the sidewalk, less than five meters from where they stood. Cars honking. A siren in the distance. Someone let out a booming laugh from the direction of the patio.

She hadn't even finished her drink. She'd forgotten all about it because this strong, gorgeous man wanted her. Kept looking at her like she was a plate of the world's tastiest dumplings and he wished to put her in his month.

She gasped. Would he want to do that?

"So, what do you say?" he asked.

It wasn't just that he was clearly attracted to her. She'd said weird things, as she sometimes did in unfamiliar situations, and he wasn't bothered by any of it. Everything seemed to roll right off him—she bet he wasn't an anxious mess half the time, unlike her. He'd also paid careful attention to her pleasure.

If she refused to go home with him, she figured he'd take it in stride. He didn't seem like the sort to get mad and say she'd been leading him on.

But although Rose had never gone home with a guy she'd just met, had never really envisioned it happening, she wanted this. Oh, she did.

And she could have it.

Better to go to his place than hers. She had a roommate, who'd be getting home around now, and Sierra wouldn't judge her, but it still seemed simpler not to have to deal with it.

"Yes," she said. "Let's go back to your place."

His grin promised all sorts of wicked things. Rose felt like she must be dreaming—this was *not* the sort of thing that happened to her.

"I just have to text my roommate so she won't worry," she told Cal.

The first night that Sierra had spent with Jake, she hadn't answered any texts because her phone had died. Rose had been worried sick, and she didn't want her roommate to feel that anxiety now.

"Want my address so she knows where you are?" Cal asked.

Rose nodded. "Thank you."

She texted Sierra, and then Cal grabbed her hand and they headed toward the subway. His fingers were still wet. From her moisture.

Just that was enough to make her breathing ragged.

Cal's basement apartment was half an hour away by transit.

"I get reduced rent," he explained, "to take care of the yard and check on the old lady upstairs a couple of times a week."

Rose was barely processing his words as he led her inside.

"Sorry, I wasn't expecting company," he said.

"That's okay." She'd lived in much worse conditions at the

lowest point of her depression. His place wasn't neat, but it certainly wasn't filthy.

But her brain wasn't focused on that.

When he moved to kiss her after she slipped off her shoes, she stepped back.

"You okay?" he asked in a concerned voice.

She was now more anxious than excited, that was the problem.

"I, uh, haven't done anything like this before," she said.

His brows knit together. "You've never had sex?"

"I have. A bunch of times. Just never gone home with someone from a bar, and I don't have a lot of experience."

"We don't have to. We could play video games, or if you'd rather leave…"

As soon as he said it, she realized just how much she wanted this night with him.

"No, no," she said, looking up at him as she moved closer. "I only wanted you to know that I don't really know what I'm doing."

"Just let me make you feel good."

"And now everything's weird and I've ruined the mood."

"Nah, it's all fine." He put a hand on her shoulder and stroked it, the pad of his thumb gently moving back and forth.

This guy really didn't seem bothered by anything. What would that be like?

He led her to the bedroom, and when he tackled her onto the queen-size bed, she laughed.

"Too bad I don't have one of those corset things," he said. "I really would be happy to see you in that."

"So, what are you going to do instead?"

Oh my. Did her voice sound sassy? Flirtatious?

Whatever it was, it wasn't like her.

"Get you naked," he said simply.

She felt a moment of nervousness when he pulled her dress

over her head, followed by her bra. It had been a long time since she'd been naked around anyone. But those feelings soon fled as he ran his hands all over her body, like he couldn't get enough of her, and fastened his lips to her nipple.

She hadn't realized she enjoyed nipple play so much. Not until tonight.

And now that they were all alone, she could get him naked, too. She pulled off his T-shirt and tossed it on the floor, reveling in the chance to touch him everywhere, from his strong muscles down to the slight swell of his stomach.

Yeah, he was certainly gorgeous, and she pressed her thighs together.

As his mouth moved lower and lower, he tugged off her panties, but before he could set his mouth between her legs, she jerked up. "Wait!"

He lifted his head. "Not your thing?"

"I think it could be, but I've never done it before."

"No one's ever gone down on you?"

She shook her head. Though she'd had penetrative sex with three guys, she'd never received oral sex. She'd asked one of them, but he hadn't been into it.

"Well, that's a shame," Cal said. "You want to try it tonight? I'm game if you are." The corner of his mouth kicked up.

"Yeah." She lay down, anticipation now overtaking her nerves.

He bent his head again and gave her pussy one long, slow lick. The sensation was a little odd, but in a good way.

Next, he licked her clit, which was even better.

She lost track of what he did after that; she just knew that it felt really, really good. As wonderful as she'd imagined it would feel—no. Even better. She gripped the sheets and bucked her hips toward his face.

Dear God. She'd never gotten close to orgasm this quickly before.

Rose squeezed her eyes shut and concentrated on the sensations coursing through her body. She even found herself pinching her nipples as her breath quickened.

"Cal!" she cried out, unable to stop herself.

He crawled up her body with a satisfied look on his face, and then he kissed her.

Since no one had ever gone down on her before, no one else had kissed her when her moisture was on their lips. It turned her on, this proof that he'd had his head buried between her legs. She pulled him close, his hairy chest against her, and groaned into his mouth.

Oh, yes. This was going to be a good night.

She fumbled with his belt, shoved down his shorts and boxers, and took his cock in her hand. It seemed sizable.

He hissed out a breath, and it delighted her how much he liked her touch.

With her other hand, she pulled out his hair elastic and set it on the bedside table. "I love your long hair," she said as she ran her fingers through it.

He rolled over and lay on his back next to her. "I hope you love other parts, too."

"Oh, yeah. Your baby toe. Your pinky finger. Your..." She laughed when he slid his smallest finger inside her.

"You were saying?" he asked.

"I told you I like it!"

He removed his finger when she slid downward and licked his cock. She lifted her gaze to watch his face, and the heat in those brown eyes...it nearly undid her. Although she'd come not long before, she was aching for him to fill her.

He was already reaching for a condom.

Good. She watched eagerly as he raised himself up on his knees and rolled it on. He looked strong. Powerful. Capable of bringing her even more pleasure than he already had.

For a split second, she felt like she was watching this scene unfold from far away. It was still hard to believe it was really happening to her. She was in this hot guy's bed, and he was preparing to fuck her.

Her inner muscles clenched.

"Cal," she moaned, now very much in the moment.

She lay on her back, and he lowered himself on one arm, using his other hand to guide his cock to her entrance.

"You good?" he asked, his voice unsteady, as he began pushing inside.

"Yeah."

Though he wasn't all the way inside her yet, she already felt very, very full.

But she took more of him.

And more.

And when he started thrusting, her eyes practically rolled to the back of her head.

Oh, yes, she was very, very, *very* good.

She clutched his back, loving his weight on top of her, and kissed him; his lips still tasted faintly of her juices, and that was still a turn-on, though how anything could make her more aroused when she was practically vibrating with pleasure, she had no idea.

She wrapped her leg around his and lifted her hips to meet his over and over again.

"You feel fucking amazing," he said.

Rose, on the other hand, was at a complete loss for words. She just held him tightly and kissed him and met his thrusts, her body building toward its inexorable release.

When he came at the same time as her, growling in her ear, she was suffused with joy.

She couldn't remember the last time she'd felt so close to someone.

Rose wasn't quite sure what was supposed to happen now, but she did know that she should use the washroom to prevent a UTI, and when she came back, she was more conscious of her nakedness than she'd been a few minutes ago.

Cal took his turn in the bathroom, and then he returned to bed and wrapped an arm around her. He had a dopey smile on his face, and his hair was a bit frizzy. She still thought he looked absolutely gorgeous naked, but she was no longer consumed by desperation.

Now, she could enjoy him in other ways. She curled up and rested her head on his chest.

"How was doing something you'd never done before?" he asked.

"Ten out of ten, would do it again."

He pulled her closer, and suddenly, there were tears in her eyes. Being in his arms when she was used to being alone…this just felt so damn nice. It was a relief to be able to touch someone like this.

But she didn't want to seem unstable, so she refused to let those tears fall; she was practiced at holding back her tears, after all.

"You want to stay the night?" he asked.

"Yes."

"Would you like something to wear to bed, or are you good sleeping naked?"

"A shirt would be nice."

He walked toward the dresser, completely unselfconscious in his nudity. She wondered what it would be like to have this view every day. To be that lucky.

He tossed her a plain white T-shirt, which smelled of laundry soap. She pulled it over her head; it wasn't too tight, even if she was hardly a small woman.

And though five minutes ago, she'd been on the verge of tears, now she felt like laughing. She'd actually had a one-night stand and—

Wait. Was this a one-night stand?

She didn't like the idea.

It was rare for her to feel this kind of connection with someone. She'd grown up thinking that when she was older, she'd go on tons of dates. On sitcoms like *Friends*, the characters always seemed to be going on dates with someone new.

But her life hadn't been like that.

In the back of her mind, she couldn't help worrying that what Cal wanted and what she wanted were very different things. Usually that anxiety would snowball, but perhaps due to all the orgasms and the warm comfort of his presence, she was able to keep those thoughts at bay.

And a little while later, she enjoyed yet another orgasm.

[4]

AT THREE IN THE MORNING, Rose's brain was in full swing. The boneless contentedness she'd felt a few hours ago had completely disappeared as the reality of insomnia set in.

She had the impression that some people slept easily after an orgasm or four. And some people slept easily when they were tired.

Unfortunately, Rose wasn't "some people."

There wasn't much correlation between how tired she was and how long it took her to fall asleep, and there were a number of things that were working against her right now.

The first was that she was in an unfamiliar bed without her plushies to snuggle. She could snuggle up to Cal…but that brought her to the second problem.

Not only was this an unfamiliar bed, but it was an unfamiliar bed with someone else in it. She had precious little experience with sharing a bed, and it had never gone well for her in the past. But when Cal had suggested she stay the night, all those memories had flown out of her brain, and she'd readily agreed.

She didn't think he'd mind a cuddle, but for a number of reasons, she doubted that would work for her. He radiated heat like a furnace, and it was August. Also, he was a very different size from a plushie. And lastly, if she got closer to him, his snoring would be even louder.

Yup, he snored. Quiet snores, but still. Those sounds set her teeth on edge, especially since she didn't have her white-noise machine.

Another thing that was possibly keeping her awake? The fact that she hadn't taken her antidepressant, which she usually took near bedtime. She didn't have her meds with her because she hadn't expected to spend the night away from home. That hadn't occurred to her when she'd decided they should go to his place rather than hers.

Rose went to the washroom again and returned to bed.

Once again, it didn't wake Cal.

Unlike her, he seemed to easily fall asleep and stay asleep. He was the kind of guy whose brain wasn't whirring a thousand kilometers an hour in the middle of the night. How lucky.

When he released another snore, louder than the others, she clenched her fists. Dammit, this was unbearable.

What was wrong with her? Why couldn't she sleep?

You know why you can't sleep, Rose. You just went through a long list of reasons.

Alright. Time to remove herself from this situation. The longer she stayed in bed, wide awake, the more broken she felt. It had already been three hours.

She tiptoed out of his bedroom, closed the door, and used her phone's flashlight to find the light switch in the living room. There was no blanket on the couch, but the sweatshirt on the coffee table would be good enough. She couldn't sleep if she wasn't covered by some kind of blanket.

She looked at her phone for a few minutes. Just pictures of plushies on Instagram—nothing that would get her too worked up. Then she turned out the light and tried to get some shut-eye.

But her mind was still whirring. She wasn't even sure *what* it was whirring with, but despite being exhausted and no longer having to listen to Cal's snoring, she was wide awake, tears silently streaming down her face.

Yep, she was crying. It was a regular occurrence when she couldn't sleep. Fortunately, she'd slept pretty well for the past few months, but now she seemed to be making up for lost time.

The one night she'd gone home with a guy!

Oh, God, she was such a mess. How could she ever have a long-term relationship when she acted like this? Who'd want to date her?

Usually, she was better at stopping herself from spiraling, but it was always particularly tough in the middle of the night when she couldn't sleep, and the fact that she was in an unfamiliar situation only aggravated that.

Part of the problem was that many people believed someone like Rose shouldn't date. She was mentally ill, which meant she should "work on herself first." But she *had* worked on herself, and the past few years were the best she'd had as an adult.

Maybe that wasn't enough. It would never be enough. She was just too much of a mess—

Bright lights came on, and she squeezed her eyes shut.

"Rose?" Cal said. "I heard you get up."

Oh, no. This was just getting worse.

He came to sit on the couch beside her. "Are you crying?"

She opened her eyes since there was no sense trying to hide it now.

"What's wrong?" he asked. "Do you regret it? I know you said it was something you hadn't done before."

He wore a T-shirt and boxers, and even when she was viewing him through bleary eyes at three thirty in the morning, he looked good.

"No," she said. "I had fun. I'm just not used to sleeping away from home."

"Do you want me to drive you to your place?"

"It's the middle of the night. You don't need to do that."

"Just give me a few minutes to wake up and—"

"No, no. It's fine."

He frowned. "What do you need to sleep?"

"I don't know, but you snore—"

"I'll sleep on the couch, then. You can have the bed."

She couldn't kick him out of his bed in his own home, especially when he was such a big guy—it would be particularly uncomfortable on the couch for him.

"Do you have a white-noise machine or a not-so-quiet fan?" she asked. "What about a stuffed animal? I usually have something to hold when I sleep."

"You can snuggle up to me."

"You're too big and warm. It's not the same."

"Fair enough." He stood up. "Let me show you what I've got."

She followed him into his bedroom, where he pulled a small fan out of the closet. He plugged it in and turned it on, and she was pleased with the result. That should prevent his snores from setting her teeth on edge. Then he reached into his night table and took out a teddy bear in a Blue Jays jersey.

"How's this?" He handed it to her.

She wrapped her arms around the bear. "He'll do."

"Cool."

That was it. One word and a smile.

He didn't seem terribly bothered that she was a weird insomniac who liked plushies. Didn't say anything about her being too old for stuffed animals. Didn't make a big deal out of her behavior, which was probably nothing like that of the women he'd brought home in the past.

They got into bed together, and he pulled her close for a moment and kissed her on the cheek like it was the natural thing to do.

"Goodnight again," he said. "Wake me if you need anything else."

And with that, he rolled over and promptly fell asleep.

Rose squeezed the teddy bear tight. Her brain wasn't going haywire like it had half an hour ago. This didn't feel quite like home, but it should be good enough.

And, indeed, it was.

Rose opened her eyes and looked around the room.

Yep, last night had definitely happened.

She was in a basement apartment, not her upstairs bedroom, and she was wearing another person's shirt and hugging another person's teddy bear. The alarm clock on the bedside table said it was nine, which mean she'd had at least five hours of sleep. Not great, but no big deal as long as it wasn't happening multiple days in a row.

She got out of the unfamiliar bed and walked into the kitchen, where Cal was drinking coffee and looking at something on his phone. He was big and beautiful in the small amount of morning light coming through the tiny basement windows.

"Hey, you're up." He smiled.

"Sorry about the middle of the night…" She trailed off because somehow, his smile told her that it didn't matter. He just seemed happy to see her.

"You sleep okay after that?" he asked. "I didn't want to wake you."

"Yeah. I slept fine."

He got up and walked to the coffeemaker. "Coffee?"

"Sure."

"Can I make you anything for breakfast?"

She wasn't used to this morning-after business. Did the other person usually offer to make you breakfast? He wasn't rushing her out the door, which was nice.

She noticed a loaf of bread on the counter. "Toast? With peanut butter or jam, whatever you have."

"I've got both."

"Both is good."

He handed her a mug of coffee. Their hands brushed in the process, and…mmm. Even if they'd gone much further than brushing hands yesterday, the little touch was still pretty thrilling. Almost as thrilling as the fact that he was smiling at her, unbothered by her crying and insomnia last night.

She hovered as he put bread in the toaster and got out the peanut butter and jam. It seemed weird for someone else to make toast for her, but she let him. It was his kitchen.

When her toast was ready, she finally took a seat, munching her food and drinking her coffee in silence. It was a slightly awkward silence, but she had the odd feeling that silence could quickly become comfortable with him.

"You have some jam right here." He pointed to his top lip, then reached forward.

"Do I really?" she asked. "Or do you just want a reason to touch me?"

Who *was* she?

He barked out a laugh. Then his expression sobered and he said, softly, "Does it matter?"

"No," she said, "it doesn't."

He leaned forward, wiped her upper lip, and kissed her, a kiss that quickly became as needy as their touches last night. He pulled her up to standing, then picked her up and carried her to bed.

Yep, this was certainly a good way to wake up.

Afterward, she put on her red dress and made sure she had everything in her purse. Her hands were shaking a little.

What will happen now?

She followed Cal to the front door.

"I had a really great time with you," he said. "Glad I met you at the bar."

Something suddenly occurred to her. "Your friend! You were waiting for him."

"I texted him and let him know I'd met someone and I'd see him some other time. He was with his girlfriend—I'm sure he didn't mind." Cal paused. "How about you give me your number, and I'll take you out next weekend? You interested?"

"Yes!" She grinned goofily, and he returned her grin.

He pulled his phone out of his pocket, and she dictated her number.

He nodded. "Alright, I'll text you."

"Sounds good." She tilted her head up and pressed one last kiss to his lips. After putting on her sandals, she practically skipped up the steps to the sidewalk.

She'd met someone last night! He was very good in bed, and he was hot and kind and easygoing…and he really liked her! He wanted to see her again!

She twirled on the sidewalk before texting Sierra to let her know she'd be home soon.

Cal felt like he was forgetting something. Did he have plans later today?

It was just hard to think of anything except what had happened last night.

Rose, coming on his hand against a brick wall.

Rose, clutching his hair and bucking against his face as he licked her.

Rose's mouth parting as he slid into her.

Rose's look of delight when he handed her a teddy bear.

Rose, Rose, Rose.

He wanted to see her again. He wasn't a complicated guy and—

Shit! He was supposed to have lunch with his parents. That was what he'd forgotten. He was supposed to be there in—he looked at his phone—fifteen minutes, and it was a twenty-minute drive.

Shit.

His dad would be pissed, but what else was new? Dad was always unhappy with him. It shouldn't bother Cal anymore, since it had been like this forever, but although few things got him worked up, Dad was one of them.

The drive itself wasn't too bad, but when Cal got to his parents' street, it looked like someone nearby was having a Sunday brunch party, based on the lack of street parking. After driving around the block a couple of times, he finally managed to find a spot.

Now twenty minutes late, he jumped out of the car and started running toward his parents' house, but a *thunk* made him stop and turn around.

His phone had fallen out of his pocket.

He was about to run back and pick it up, but then he saw a moving truck barreling toward him, and he leaped out of the way.

And watched in horror as the truck ran over his phone.

The phone was almost four years old, and he'd been meaning to get a new one.

But what about Rose's number?

[5]

"You're late." Dad made a show of checking his watch after opening the front door. "Half an hour late."

"Yeah, sorry about that," Cal said. "I left a little later than I should have, and then—"

"What's in the shopping bag?" Kendall, his fifteen-year-old niece, gestured to the bag in his hand.

"A truck ran over my phone. Those are the pieces."

"Oh. That sucks." Her eyes returned to her own phone as she wandered into the living room.

Dad, on the other hand, shot Cal his *only-you-could-do-a-thing-like-that* look, which normally might get under Cal's skin a little, but he couldn't help thinking about Rose. Would he still be able to contact her? Could he recover her number somehow?

"You think you're going to reassemble your phone from... that?" Dad asked, peering into the bag.

"No." But Cal had gathered up the fragments just in case.

Because, dammit, he really did want to see Rose again, and he wasn't sure how he could do that if he didn't have her number.

His sister, Jodi, entered the front hall along with her husband and their youngest daughter, Riley.

"Uncle Cal, you were supposed to come early so we could play catch!" Riley was eleven, and normally Cal would be more than happy to play catch with her, but he was distracted at present.

He patted her shoulder. "After lunch, okay?" It would delay buying a new phone, but he wouldn't disappoint her. "Where's Jed?"

"They're on vacation," Jodi said.

Right. Cal remembered that now. His brother and family had taken a trip to the Maritimes before the kids went back to school. Cal was the youngest of three, and his brother and sister were both quite a bit older than him—they were in their forties.

He headed into the kitchen and waited to hug his mother until she'd taken the quiche out of the oven. Mushroom quiche, from the looks of it "Smells great, Mom."

"You're here!" she said. "I was starting to worry. Bad traffic?"

"Nah, not too bad."

She frowned, and he turned away, listening to the argument that had broken out elsewhere in the house. Jodi and Kendall were often arguing these days. On a few occasions, Kendall had wanted space from her mom and had stayed at Cal's for a night.

Five minutes later, they all sat down to eat in the dining room, and Dad asked Cal about work. Cal knew his father wasn't actually curious, though. Dad had no respect for what his youngest child, the family disappointment, did with his life, and so Cal didn't bother giving much of an answer as he scarfed down his food. The faster he ate, the sooner he could play catch with Riley and get a new phone.

Except nobody else was eating as fast as he was, and Mom was looking at him oddly.

"You sure you're okay, honey?" she asked.

"Yeah, I'm good," Cal said with an easy smile that didn't match how he felt, then slowed his pace.

Dad appeared skeptical but didn't speak.

Cal never talked to his dad on the phone—or texted him, for

that matter. He maintained a distant relationship with his father mainly for the sake of his mom and the rest of the family, and when Dad criticized him for one thing or another, Cal didn't bother standing up for himself and tried not to let the older man's words get to him.

What was Rose's family like?

His thoughts drifted back to her and that radiant smile she'd given him this morning. He usually felt calmer than he did now, but with his dad glaring at him and Rose on his mind, he wasn't his usual self.

Well, so it went. He'd just have to do his best to get through this family meal.

"Tell me everything," Sierra said as soon as Rose stepped in the door.

"I need to shower and change my clothes and brush my teeth."

"But *then* you're telling me everything."

Rose nodded, still feeling a little giddy.

Upstairs in the shower, she soaped herself up, and touching her skin felt different from usual. She tipped her head back in the spray and smiled. She was *present* in her body. Appreciative of it.

She took her time moisturizing her skin before she threw on some clothes and went downstairs, where Sierra had made a pot of tea.

"How was your trip up north?" Rose asked as she poured herself a cup.

Sierra gave her a look.

"I'm kidding!" Rose said. "I know you want to hear about last night." She had a sip of tea. "I didn't feel like staying in, so I went out for dinner, then figured I'd have a drink at Nautilus. You know the table under the blimp? I left my cardigan there to save my spot while I got a drink, but when I returned, *he* was sitting there. Big white guy named Cal. I was a little pissed at him, then I acted a bit awkward."

She continued describing the evening, leaving out the part where he'd gotten her off in public—Rose still couldn't believe that had been her—and glossing over the details of the sex, except to say it was good and…

"You know how I'd never…"

"Oh my God!" Sierra said. "He went down on you."

Rose blushed. "More than once."

"Did you like it?"

"Yeah. A lot." Rose also glossed over just how upset she'd been in the middle of the night, moving on to the events of the morning. "We ate breakfast, had sex again." She spoke as though it was no big deal, even though before last night, it had been years since she'd been intimate with a guy. "He asked for my number and said he'd take me out next weekend."

"That's amazing," Sierra said. "I'm really happy for you."

Rose smiled. She was happy for herself, too.

She checked her phone. Cal hadn't texted her yet, but that was fine. She'd left his home an hour ago. It was probably uncool to text someone immediately, and she might have slept with Cal, but she didn't know him all that well. Not well enough to know what his texting habits were. She wouldn't worry yet, even if she was particularly prone to worrying.

Nope, she'd just trust that he'd text her in the next couple of days.

He would, wouldn't he?

$$[\ 6\ ]$$

"How was your weekend?" Rose's father asked on Monday night.

Rose paused the show she'd been watching and settled back on the couch for the phone call. "Not too exciting."

By Rose's standards, the weekend had been quite exciting, but it wasn't the sort of thing she could talk to her father about. Though if Cal had already texted, she might have said, *I met a guy. I've got a date next weekend.*

Although she kept telling herself that it hadn't been forty-eight hours yet and he would text her eventually, her doubts were starting to creep in.

"Rose?" Dad said. "Are you okay?"

"Yeah." She paused. "I'm just a bit…lonely."

"I know you'll say I'm biased—"

She chuckled.

"—but you will find someone."

Her father thought the world of her. Sometimes it was hard to voice her fears to him—she didn't feel like he could really understand—but it was better to have someone who was always in her corner than the alternative, of course.

She switched the subject. "You're still retiring? You haven't changed your mind?"

"No, I haven't changed my mind in the last two days," he said, and she could hear his smile through the phone. "It's time."

They spoke for a few more minutes, and then Rose returned to comfort-watching *The Untamed*.

~

By Thursday, Cal still hadn't texted, and Rose couldn't avoid obsessing over it.

He was the one who'd asked for her number. He wouldn't have done that if he wasn't interested in more, right? Or had he asked just because he knew it was what she'd hoped to hear? That didn't seem like Cal, but she reminded herself again that she hardly knew him.

Had he intended to ask her out, then decided that on second thought, he didn't want to be with a woman who'd blurted out that she had an Instagram account for her stuffed alpaca?

What's wrong with me? Am I unlovable?

Her dad loved her. His actions told her that—and his words did, too. But that was a different sort of love.

Cal's never going to contact me, is he?

It had been more than ninety-six hours, and he'd said he wanted to take her out this coming weekend. Wouldn't he have texted by now if he really intended to do that?

Yeah, she wasn't going to hear from him.

She asked herself if her pessimism was "just her depression talking," but that sent her on another spiral.

Damn.

~

Saturday evening, Rose got ready to go to Ossington Cider Bar. She put on jeans and a cute top, but it didn't make her feel pretty.

She'd debated not going out with her friends. She just wasn't in the mood.

But what else would she do? Wallow at home?

She and Sierra walked to the bar, where they met up with Charlotte and Nicole. Amy was pregnant and not feeling great, and she'd decided to skip tonight.

"So, Rose," Nicole said, waggling her eyebrows once they all had a pint of cider in hand, "tell me about the guy you met."

Right. Rose had texted Nicole about Cal last Sunday, but now, she didn't feel like sharing the details she'd shared with Sierra.

"I never heard from him," Rose said.

"Bastard," Charlotte muttered. "Fucking bastard."

"He's one of those guys who just enjoys stringing women along," Nicole said. "Bastard is right. You're better off without him. If he were here, I'd force-feed him a whole bowl of those Brussels sprouts that Sierra keeps inexplicably ordering. Without the cheese and bacon."

"Maybe he has good taste and likes Brussels sprouts," Sierra said. "I mean, he chose Rose—"

"And never texted her," Nicole said. "Don't worry, Rose. We'll find you someone else."

"Thanks." Rose didn't really believe it would happen, though.

"You know where he lives, don't you?" Charlotte asked. "We could, like, egg his house. Demand that he explain himself."

That was true. Rose *did* know where Cal lived, but by not contacting her, he'd made his feelings clear. What was the point in going back there? She'd seem like a stalker.

Conversation moved on to other topics, and Rose forced herself to participate in the conversation and laugh at the appropriate times, but she wasn't really into it.

That night, she went home and snuggled her plushies as she cried silently into the pillow.

He's just a guy. We spent a single night together.

But that sort of thing was unusual for Rose. She wasn't one of those sitcom characters who were always going on dates. She wasn't like Nicole, who oozed sex appeal and used to sleep around a lot, back before she'd met David Cho. No, she was more like Charlotte, who hadn't dated at all for five years after her ex. Charlotte had actually sworn off dating, but it wasn't as if she'd had many interested men in that time, even though she was pretty awesome.

Rose had felt like she and Cal had something special. When he'd kissed her, when he'd given her a teddy bear to cuddle like it was no big deal, when he'd handed her that mug of coffee and their fingers brushed…

But really, she'd just spent one night with him. Why couldn't she stop obsessing over this bastard, as Charlotte had called him?

Because you're such a mess. You're a loser and nobody—

She cut off the voice in her head. It was a liar. There were lots of great people in the world who wanted lasting relationships but weren't lucky enough to have one. It didn't mean there was anything wrong with her.

That was what she would say to a friend in this situation.

Rose used to have faith that love would happen to her eventually, but it had become harder to believe that in the last year or two.

She snuggled her plushies tight and focused on her breathing. Though her mind calmed, she still didn't feel great, but she'd get through this.

She'd gotten through much worse, after all.

A few minutes later, she picked up her phone and played Whitney Houston's "Greatest Love of All." She smiled through her tears as she remembered her mother singing along to this song while she did the dishes.

"You're sure there's no way to recover her number?" Cal asked Marv. They were in Cal's apartment that Sunday, watching the Jays game and drinking beer.

"If you'd saved it to your Google account, it would be there," Marv said. "But when you created the new contact, you must have just saved it on your phone."

After lunch with his parents, Cal had hurried over to Rogers and gotten a new phone. He'd set it up and logged into his Google account. The phone had found all the apps he'd had on his old phone, as well as some of his contacts.

But not hers.

Cal rarely swore in anger, but he'd done it last Sunday afternoon.

He still had all the pieces of his old phone at home. Perhaps someone smarter than him or Marv would know how to retrieve her number, but so far, he'd come up empty.

"And you don't, like, know her last name?" Marv asked. "That might make it easier to find her on social media."

"No," Cal said. "Though she does have an Instagram account for her alpaca."

"A *what*?"

"An Instagram account. For her stuffed alpaca."

"Yeah, I heard that part."

Cal felt a little defensive. "So what? It makes her happy."

He dropped his gaze to his new phone and pulled up Instagram. How did one find a stuffed alpaca on social media? He didn't know her alpaca's name or what it looked like, so how would he know it was hers?

Fifteen minutes later, he'd managed to find many alpaca farms and a stuffed alpaca named Sweetie Pie. Sweetie Pie was a striped alpaca based in Ireland. He'd also found a stuffed alpaca named Robbi, location unknown, but it looked tropical.

Ah, well. He'd have to give up.

He'd stopped by Nautilus last night to have a drink, just in case she decided to go there again, but he wasn't going to start going there every day, and it hadn't seemed like she went there very often anyway.

Marv cheered, and Cal glanced up. Looked like one of the Jays had hit a homerun, but Cal went back to his phone, trying to figure out what else he could do.

And then he remembered that it wasn't completely hopeless—she knew where he lived, right? When she didn't hear from him, hopefully she'd realize that he'd lost her number and come looking for him. It seemed like a bit of a longshot, but so it went.

Besides, there were lots of pretty women out there. No need to get hung up on this one just because they'd had a good night together.

His heart clenched as he thought of Rose curled up on his couch, unable to sleep.

He hoped she wasn't too upset that he hadn't texted.

[7]

As summer turned into fall, Rose pretended her mental health wasn't slipping, but it definitely was.

She went to work and did her best to keep the house clean. She talked to her father. She went out with her friends. She kept up life as usual because from her experience, that was the only way to stop herself from getting really, really bad.

But it certainly didn't mean things were *good*.

Sierra carved an elaborate trio of pumpkins for Halloween, and Rose took a cute picture of the jack-o'-lanterns with Fred, who was dressed up as a superhero with a cape and mask. She posted it on Instagram, but it didn't bring her any joy. She didn't even crack a smile at any of Penguin Pip's comments.

She was just going through the motions. Some days, she had to force herself to eat because her appetite was so poor.

Rose saw her doctor, who upped the dose of her meds, but it didn't help. She got on a list to see a psychiatrist—her old one had retired—but she didn't expect anything useful to come of that, even if she eventually got an appointment. She'd been through this whole dance before.

The main thing the mental health system had ever given her

was validation. *Yes, you are very sick.* That validation had been a profound relief for Rose: someone acknowledging she had a problem, but without acting like it was deeply shameful and all her fault.

Unfortunately, meds and therapy had never worked as well for her as they did for some people, but Rose was trying things again because she felt like she should. So she could say she'd done it.

She watched the same movies and TV shows over and over because it was comforting. Because after a whole day of work, her brain was basically unable to function. Things that weren't familiar left her confused. Words just sounded fuzzy in her brain.

She hid how bad it was from her father because she didn't want him to worry.

Fall turned to winter, and Amy had her baby. When Rose held Hudson for the first time, she didn't feel much. He was cute, and she was happy for her friend in theory...she tried not to be mad at herself for not feeling more.

She turned thirty-five, and Sierra bought her a cake.

Thirty-five and still single.

On the bright side, since Rose had no intention of birthing children, she didn't feel like she had an expiry date. She considered downloading a dating app, but maybe it wasn't the best idea when she was this depressed, especially since rejection would be particularly painful.

If only Cal had texted her...if only they'd started dating...

Would that have staved off this depressive episode?

Not that she blamed him for it, of course, and it wasn't like she'd been completely depression-free until after that night. In fact, she hadn't been depression-free for twenty years. But it went up and down, and now was definitely a low point.

Her brain tried to tell her again that she was an unlovable loser, and that was why Cal hadn't texted her. She couldn't keep those thoughts away.

Her concentration became so poor that she considered taking a leave of absence from work, since she was struggling to do her job, but she really didn't want to do that. Just arranging it and getting a note from her doctor…it felt like too much effort. And what would she do all day? Plus, she liked feeling productive at work, though her self-worth shouldn't depend on her productivity.

Eventually, Rose's father figured out how unwell she was. He immediately drove to Toronto, all the way from Ottawa, and knocked on her door at one in the morning. She'd told him it wasn't necessary, but to him, it was very necessary.

He'd lost his severely depressed wife to suicide, after all.

Rose desperately wanted to get better so he'd stop worrying about her, but if she'd been able to will her way out of depression, it would have already happened a thousand times over.

In March, Rose stuffed Fred into her purse and went to Harbord Coffee Bar, where she got a coffee and a slice of roll cake. And for some reason, as she took a picture of Fred smiling by the window —Fred always smiled; he couldn't seem to do otherwise—she found herself smiling a little, too.

She wasn't forcing herself to smile. She was just…smiling.

She still felt heavy inside, but it was like she was carrying a twenty-pound bag of rice on her chest rather than a hundred-pound bag, which was a significant improvement. The ability to feel the tiniest bit of pleasure was certainly nice.

A week later, Rose was reading on the couch and snuggling her sloth plushie when Sierra sat down beside her.

"I want to talk to you about something," Sierra said.

Rose straightened and put aside her e-reader. "What's up?"

Sierra twisted her hands and looked oddly nervous.

"What is it?" Rose asked again, afraid something bad had happened.

"I want to move in with Jake."

Oh. Rose knew how this conversation would proceed.

"But you haven't been well lately," Sierra continued, "so maybe it's not the best time…"

"No, no." The last thing Rose wanted was to hold her friends back. It would make her feel terribly guilty. "But I guess I'll have to find a new roommate."

The thought was utterly exhausting, but moving would be even worse. She simply didn't have the executive function to coordinate a move right now.

"Amy and I will interview people," Sierra said. Amy owned the house—she'd inherited it from her great aunt—and now lived next door with her husband. "If we find someone appropriate, you can meet them and give your final approval."

Rose burst into tears. She honestly hadn't cried in months—she was often too numb to cry—but now she couldn't help it.

Over the next few weeks, she kept telling herself that the roommate situation would turn out okay. She trusted Sierra and Amy to find someone nice, but that didn't mean this person would become her friend. And she was determined not to show her new housemate the full extent of her issues.

She waited for news of prospective housemates, but she didn't hear anything until a month later, when she was spending two weeks in Ottawa with her family. It was her second day there, and she'd just met her twin baby nephews for the first time.

"We found someone!" Sierra said over the phone. "You said you were okay with a male housemate, right?"

"Yes," Rose replied.

"His name is Caleb Dempsey. We called his last landlord, an elderly grandma, and she had such nice things to say. We met him…do you want to meet him, too, before you agree?"

Rose considered this. It would probably be the smart thing to do, but she was in Ottawa for a while, and the idea of having one more thing to figure out was almost overwhelming. It shouldn't be, but it was.

She could have her friends handle this for her.

"No, I trust you," she said.

When she left Ottawa, after the longest break she'd had in almost a year, she felt a little better. She did seem to be on an upward swing. At least she wasn't getting worse and wondering how much worse it could get.

Because things could always get worse. That was just a fact of life.

On the drive back to Toronto, she wondered if it was time to think about trying dating apps. She still, on occasion, felt guilty for wanting a relationship. She felt like she was supposed to be enough for herself.

She banished those thoughts. Nothing wrong with wanting romance, was there?

But that didn't necessarily mean she should pursue it. Dating seemed like so much effort, and there were so many opportunities for pain. Hoping and then having your hopes dashed—that was awful.

She'd gone through it when she'd decided to get help for her depression after moving to Toronto, determined that she wouldn't end her own life like her mother had. When the doctor had written a prescription for an antidepressant, Rose had been in a bad state, and she'd desperately clung to the idea that it could lift this horrible weight off her chest.

It hadn't. It had just given her side effects.

She'd hoped when she'd tried the next one, too, but by the time she got to the third, she realized it was less painful not to hope. That way, she wouldn't be as crushed when it didn't work.

Still, she'd foolishly hoped again the first time she'd tried therapy for her depression, perhaps because she'd seen a grief counselor in Ottawa and that had helped with processing her grief. Rose forced herself through four sessions of cognitive behavioral therapy before realizing the therapist just didn't get her, though who was she to judge? Maybe her judgment was skewed because of her depression.

So she'd gone to another two sessions before giving up on that one, and it had taken her months to try therapy again—and that therapist had ended up being fatphobic. Her psychiatrist at the time had seemed insistent that CBT should work, and Rose did benefit a little from the sessions with her third therapist. At some point, however, she decided she'd gotten as much out of CBT as she could, a decision she'd constantly second-guessed. One day, she'd try a different type of talk therapy, but she wasn't sure which kind would be best, and those unsuccessful attempts had taken so much out of her.

By her seventh antidepressant, Rose was trying meds just to say she'd tried them. But that one worked...a small amount. Maybe twenty percent, but by that point, she'd figured it was the best she could expect, so that was the one she'd stayed on.

She'd also tried electroconvulsive therapy, which provided relief for many people with treatment-resistant depression, but it hadn't helped her. Plus, it had cognitive side effects.

Navigating the mental health system was so much effort, especially when she could barely function thanks to depression, and the dashed hopes reminded her a little of Cal. They'd had a great night, and he'd said he would text her and take her out. He'd made her hope.

And then he'd never texted.

The fact that she'd been so sure they had something, so sure he meant it... That had made the fall worse. The crushing disappointment. She'd obsessed over it. Why hadn't he contacted her? Where had she gone wrong? She hadn't wanted to be so hurt over a guy she barely knew, but her heart hadn't been able to help itself.

If she wanted to try dating, really putting herself out there, she had to get some armor first. Rose was a bit like a snail without a shell at times, but that shell was important.

Being rejected right away wasn't so bad. Though it didn't feel good, it was bearable. But at some point, if she got close to a guy, she'd have to tell him about her mental illness, and if it failed then…well, that would be worse.

She wanted a relationship, but it seemed like there was so much pain baked into the process. Yet she couldn't help *wanting*.

It was in Rose's nature to be a bit hopeful, and she didn't want to completely destroy that part of herself. She'd allow herself to hope…a little.

But not too much. Not like she had with Cal.

On the first of May, Rose was reading upstairs with Fred and looking out the window every two minutes. Her new housemate was supposed to arrive any minute with a moving truck.

She hoped they'd get along, and he'd do all his chores, and they could occasionally watch movies together. It was nice to have someone around, and living with another person would force her to do her own chores and not just let everything go.

She'd put away some of the plushies on her bed, just in case he saw inside her room and thought it was weird that a thirty-five-year-old woman had twenty plushies.

"But it's not weird, is it?" she murmured, stroking Fred's head.

Just then, a car drove up and slowed in front of the house. The driver smoothly parallel parked into a nearby spot.

Yes, unfortunately, her new roommate would have to park on the street. There was only enough room for one car in the ramshackle garage out back, and that was where Rose kept her car. Sierra and Amy had told him about the parking situation, and he'd apparently been unbothered by it.

Rose, on the other hand, wouldn't deal well with street parking. Not because she sucked at parallel parking—she was actually pretty good at it—but it was a pain to look for a spot, and digging out her car in winter would be the worst.

Yeah, this guy sounded more easygoing than her.

She watched as he got out of his car. He was a big guy, with long brown hair tied back in a ponytail.

She froze. Was that…?

No, it couldn't be.

Amy came out of the house next door, Hudson in her arms, and handed the guy a key. It looked like they were laughing, and there was something about the way he moved…

Rose hurried downstairs, arriving at the entrance just as the door opened.

It was, indeed, Cal.

$$[\ 8\ ]$$

"Rose," Cal said, smiling.

When Sierra and Amy had mentioned that his new housemate would be their friend Rose, he'd immediately thought of the woman he'd met at Nautilus last summer. Could it be her? He'd quickly pushed the thought aside, figuring the probability was low. Not that Cal knew anything about probability, but still. It seemed unlikely.

Yet here she was.

It wasn't like he'd been hung up on her for the past seven or nine months, or whatever it was. But occasionally, he'd thought of that night fondly and wondered what might have been. He was pleased to see her again, and she was just as pretty as he remembered.

She was also furious.

"*You.*" She pointed her finger at him. Her other hand held a stuffed animal—was that her alpaca?—against her hip. "I thought my new housemate was Caleb."

He toed off his shoes. "Cal. For Caleb."

"I assumed it was short for Calvin."

She then said something about long vowels and short vowels…he wasn't quite following.

"You never texted me," she said. "You told me you would, but you never did."

He tried not to laugh because he knew that would piss her off, but angry Rose was rather delightful, and he really was glad to see her again.

"Why would you ask for my number," she said, "if you never intended to text me?"

"I did, but I dropped my phone and it was run over by a truck."

"That's a new one," she muttered. "Your phone was *run over by a truck*." She didn't seem to believe him. "Are you usually so careless with your phones?"

"I'd had that one for four years, but the previous one only lasted six months. I dropped it in a lake."

"I see. Did you actually drop it in a lake, or did you just say that so you didn't have to call some other poor woman you seduced?"

"You had a good time, didn't you?"

"That's not the point, Caleb."

He held up his hands. "My phone really was run over. Destroyed. When I got a new phone, I hoped to recover your number, but my friend Marv said I couldn't."

"How convenient."

"I'm not lying. I'm a pretty simple guy. If I ask for someone's number, I plan to use it. I tried to find you on social media, but I didn't know your last name, and there are lots of alpaca-related Instagram accounts, so that didn't work."

"His name is Fred," Rose said.

"Fred. Yeah, it might have helped if I'd known his name."

"Right."

She still didn't seem to believe him, but what else was he supposed to say? Had lots of men lied to her in the past? Was that the problem? There was nothing he could do about it, but he hated the thought of people being shitty to her.

"Look," she said. "Maybe a guy not texting when he said he would is no big deal to you. Maybe you're like Joey in *Friends* and have no trouble finding women to sleep with you. You just move on to someone else. But for me…"

Her lip trembled, and he stepped forward.

"Don't touch me," she snapped.

"What does Joey have to do with this?"

She shook her head. "I wouldn't expect you to understand. You with your charming smile and your big biceps—"

"You admiring me, Rose?"

Her eyes widened and she looked embarrassed. If he thought she'd enjoy it, he'd tease her some more, but that was clearly the wrong move now.

"Some white guys love Asian women," she said, "but they usually want Asian women who are petite, not like me, and I don't want to be someone's weird fetish anyway."

He was lost. It seemed she had trouble finding dates, which he didn't understand. "You're very pretty, Rose."

Her eyes flashed with anger. "You have no right to say stuff like that, not after you asked for my number and I never heard from you again."

He didn't bother defending himself, since he didn't think it would do any good.

But even though she was angry right now, he was still happy she was his new roommate. Though he did recall hearing that it was a bad idea to sleep with your roommate. Because it could be awkward…or something. Was that right?

"I'm not sure I can live with you," she said.

Shit. This was a problem.

The moving truck would show up with all his stuff in five minutes. He'd paid first and last month's rent. If needed, he could crash with a friend or his sister for a few days—he didn't consider his parents an option—while he looked for another place. But where would he put all his furniture?

It would take a while to find something, too. He'd thought he'd lucked out when he found this rental. He liked the area, and the rent was surprisingly reasonable. Also, it included utilities, so he wouldn't have to worry about paying those separately.

He'd lived in Mrs. Weissman's basement for three years, but a few months ago, she'd decided she couldn't care for a house anymore, even with his help, and sold it before moving to a retirement home. That place had been a pretty sweet deal, and he'd thought this one sounded just as good.

Except it included a woman he'd slept with and never texted. Not on purpose, but still.

Though if she was so upset about the whole thing, that probably meant she'd really liked him. He smiled at her, which earned him a glare.

"How about this?" he said. "The moving truck is on its way, and I kinda need a place to stay. We can see how it goes for a week, and then, if you decide you can't handle it—"

"Can't *handle* it?"

Goddamn. Why did he find it hot when she was pissed at him?

She clearly wasn't interested in picking up where they'd left off, didn't even believe his story, so none of that was going to happen. But he could manage living with her. Yeah, she was cute, but so what? Wasn't like he couldn't control himself.

"I mean," he said, "if you decide I piss you off too much and it's getting in the way of your..." He gestured, trying to think of the words. "Comfort. Yes, comfort. Then I can try to find somewhere else for next month, okay? Hopefully Amy will give me last month's rent back if I do that." He'd need the money. He wasn't exactly rolling in dough, and he still had that credit card debt.

Rose pursed her lips, which reminded him of kissing her and—

No! He needed to stop thinking of that.

"Fine," she said crisply. "That's fair. I suppose it's my fault for not meeting you first, but I was up in Ottawa visiting my family."

"Your family lives in Ottawa? Did you grow up there?"

"Look, I'm not in the mood for small talk. Besides, I think I hear the moving truck."

And with that, she headed upstairs.

Rose went to her room as the movers began carrying in Cal's stuff. Cal would be carrying things, too, his biceps bulging…

She really needed to stop thinking about his muscles.

It was rare that she was actually angry at someone. Someone who wasn't her, that was; her anger and frustration were usually directed inward. But he'd claimed his phone was run over by a truck.

He was a terrible liar.

She supposed he didn't need to lie very often. He could tell the truth, and with that winning smile, he'd still get away with almost everything.

Even now, she was most angry at herself. If she'd met him before he'd moved in, then she could have told Amy to find someone else. It wouldn't have been complicated, whereas now, it was a mess.

What if he's telling the truth?

She pushed aside that thought. What was more likely: Cal simply deciding he didn't want to see her again, or him dropping his phone on the road and it being destroyed?

Definitely the former.

She might not have a wealth of experience with dating, but people not calling or texting when they said they would…that was just part of it, wasn't it? Sure, he'd seemed to enjoy himself with her, and he'd been good to her that night.

But maybe he was just a player.

Sighing, she left her room and headed to the house next door. She knocked, and Amy answered a minute later. Hudson was asleep in the carrier she had strapped to her chest.

"So, what do you think?" Amy asked excitedly, apparently oblivious to Rose's dark mood. "Isn't he nice?"

"Caleb is Cal," Rose said. "The guy I slept with who said he'd text me, then never did."

Amy's eyes widened as she beckoned Rose inside. "Are you serious? Did he tell you why?" She spoke in a hushed voice, so as not to wake the baby.

"Yeah, he had some terrible excuse. I didn't believe a word of it."

"I can't believe I was so wrong about him."

For some reason, Rose had an urge to defend Cal, but she wouldn't.

"What do you want to do?" Amy asked.

"Well, we talked about it, and he agreed to see how it goes. If it doesn't work out, he'll look for somewhere else for next month, and if you could refund his last month's rent…"

"Yeah, yeah, of course."

"I'm so sorry for being a hassle," Rose said. "The only one-night stand I've ever had…"

God, she was just so *tired,* and this was one more thing to deal with.

Hudson opened his eyes.

"Oh, hello," Amy cooed as she took him out of the carrier. "Rose, could you hold him for a minute? I just want to run to the washroom before I start nursing him."

"Sure thing."

Rose sat down on the couch in the living room, the baby in

her lap. She thought he'd be fussy if he needed to be fed, but he seemed content. For now.

She loved babies. Their toothless smiles, their soft skin, their tiny hands. Occasionally they made her sad, made her think of how she couldn't have one of her own, but today, those thoughts were taking a backseat to her living situation.

She couldn't believe she was now living with *Cal*.

[9]

THIS WASN'T the first time Cal had had a roommate. He'd moved out when he was nineteen, and until his last apartment, he'd always lived with a roommate. Toronto was expensive, and he really didn't mind living with someone. He always did his best to be a decent roommate, but with Rose, it would require extra effort.

He'd be very, very neat. He'd do thoughtful things, but nothing she'd take as romantic. And he'd spend a good amount of time away from home—and when he was home, he'd keep to his room with the door closed, when possible.

Hopefully that last part could change as she warmed up to him.

On Monday morning, Cal woke up at his usual time. When he went downstairs, Rose wasn't up yet. He made enough coffee for her, and she emerged just before he left.

"Good morning," she mumbled, bleary-eyed and beautiful.

"Good morning!"

He must have sounded a bit too enthusiastic for this time of day, as she gave him a strange look. She was dressed in office clothes—gray dress pants and a blouse.

When Cal returned from work late that afternoon, she wasn't home yet. He'd picked up some groceries yesterday, and he considered starting the food-related part of his plan today, but he didn't want to come on too strong. He had a feeling it would make Rose suspicious.

Instead, he searched for something around the house to do. The place was fairly clean, but not spotless. There were cobwebs in one of the corners, higher than she'd be able to reach, and he figured that would be a good place to start. She might not notice, but that was okay.

However, she arrived home a mere two minutes later.

"Are you…? Oh."

He turned around to look at her. "Is something wrong?"

Her shoulders slumped. "You noticed I didn't get around to doing any spring cleaning."

Crap. This seemed to make her sad.

"No judgment," he said. "I know you can't reach all the places that I can."

"Mm-hmm."

Okay, he needed a new tactic. "How about I take some pictures of you and Fred?"

"Why would you do that?"

"I looked at his Instagram account. There were no pictures of you. I figured it was because selfies were awkward and…" He trailed off, realizing he'd been wrong about this somehow.

"I could have had my former roommate take photos if I wanted-ed," Rose said. "Fred's Instagram account is human-free." She spoke as though this was only logical.

"Right, right. Well, uh, since I get up before you, I'll make enough coffee for both of us each morning. How many cups do you drink?"

"Just one. Thanks."

This wasn't going as well as he'd hoped.

He'd leave her in peace for now, then tomorrow, he'd try food.

~

Tuesday, when Rose came home and walked into the kitchen, Cal was checking on the meatloaf.

"You want some?" he asked, as if this hadn't been part of his plan. "There's lots."

Her eyebrows knit together. "What is that?"

"Meatloaf."

"Huh. I've never had meatloaf before."

That surprised him. "You want to try? It's a good one. My grandma's recipe. Ready in fifteen minutes."

"Are you sure?"

"Yeah, of course."

Finally, she smiled. "That would be great, actually. Having to figure out what to eat for dinner—it's kind of exhausting to do it every day. I'm going to get changed, then I'll be back."

She returned a few minutes later, wearing pajama pants and a tank top. Her bra strap peeked out from beneath her shirt, and he tried not to remember the time he'd gotten to take that off. He wouldn't make this weird. He could do that, right?

He served her a piece of meatloaf—not huge, but she could have seconds if she liked—along with mashed potatoes, plus boiled peas and carrots. She peered at it.

"Something wrong?" he asked. "Are you allergic to anything?"

She shook her head. "I feel very white."

"I'm sorry if—"

"No, no. There's nothing wrong. Just different from what I usually cook for myself. I look forward to trying it. Thanks."

Dinner was a little awkward but not terrible, and afterward, she insisted on doing the dishes. He would have been happy to do them himself, but he didn't want to argue with her—it seemed important to Rose to do them.

Well, things seemed to be getting better. Sort of.

∿

"So let me get this straight," Marv said, when the two of them were sitting at the bar on Thursday evening. "You slept with this chick, she's pissed you didn't text, and then she ends up being your *roommate*?"

"Something like that," Cal said mildly.

"Why didn't you text her?"

"Remember when I broke my phone?"

"Oh, right, right," Marv said. "*That's* the girl?"

"Yeah, except she doesn't believe I lost her number. So now I'm trying to win her over. Cooked her dinner on Tuesday."

"You're trying to seduce her?"

"Not that kind of dinner." Cal paused. "Meatloaf isn't a romantic dinner, is it? I searched 'Is meatloaf romantic?' on the internet, but it wasn't very helpful because I just kept getting hits about the singer."

Marv was laughing his ass off. The bastard.

"What?" Cal said. "Is it some kind of romantic sign that I should know? Is it supposed to be a…what's the word…afra—"

"Aphrodisiac," Marv supplied.

"Yeah, that one."

"I don't think anyone would consider meatloaf an aphrodisiac. Or romantic in any way. Since those weren't your intentions, I suppose it was a good choice."

"I just want her to let me stay on as a roommate."

"Why are you so keen to live with her?"

"Moving's expensive. Time consuming." Cal sipped his beer.

"Yeah, yeah, I'm sure that's all it is."

"Really!"

Okay, some part of him did hope he'd get to see what was under those blouses she wore to work every day, but he was doing his best not to think about it much.

And he had a feeling his plans were working. Rose seemed to

be warming up to him, and tomorrow, he'd casually mention that he was ordering a pizza and ask if she wanted any.

His pants tightened as he imagined her sitting on the couch beside him, in yoga pants and a tank top, her glasses perched on her nose.

But nothing was happening. She'd made that clear, and he understood.

He wished he could convince her that he'd truly meant to text her, and his phone truly had gotten run over by a truck. He didn't like her thinking he was a liar.

Ah, well. He supposed he could live with it.

Nicole threw her head back and laughed. "That's the sort of thing that would happen to *me*." She immediately sobered. "Sorry. I bet it's uncomfortable."

Rose sipped her cider. "Yeah."

It was Saturday night, and they were at Ossington Cider Bar, along with Amy, Charlotte, and Sierra.

"I feel guilty," Sierra said. "I thought he'd be a great roommate."

"No, no!" Rose assured her. "You had no way of knowing."

"Have you decided what you want to do?" Amy asked.

Rose looked down at her cider. "I think he can stay."

"That was less than enthusiastic."

Well, it was still a bit uncomfortable. When Rose saw Cal, she remembered how crushed she'd felt when he never texted. The hopes she'd pinned on him. Her fears about how she'd never be able to find someone, which had gotten worse in the wake of him destroying her hope.

But there was nothing wrong with him as a roommate. He cleaned up his messes. He wasn't loud. He made her coffee. He had nice arms—

No! Bad Rose. She wasn't supposed to think about that.

Maybe she was warming up to him because twice this past week, he'd arranged dinner. Occasionally, when she didn't feel like cooking, she ordered food, but yesterday, she hadn't needed to worry about what to order or where to order it from; she hadn't even needed to answer the door.

So, yeah, she supposed he could stay. She'd feel guilty about making him find another place to live, when really it was her fault for not meeting him beforehand, even if he'd failed to text her last summer.

Rose drained the rest of her cider. "I'll be right back." She headed to the washroom.

When she was returning to her table, she tripped...on her own two feet.

Oh, dear. She wasn't usually this clumsy. She hurtled toward the floor, braced for impact, but it never happened.

Instead, she found herself in someone's arms.

"You okay?" a low voice murmured.

"Uh, yeah."

Slowly, she straightened up and took a look at her rescuer. An East Asian guy in dress pants and a black shirt, his dark hair a bit spiky.

Good-looking? Definitely.

He smiled at her, and she smiled back hesitantly, unsure of what to do in such a situation. A man had literally saved her. She likely wouldn't have ended up with more than a bruised knee and bruised pride, but still.

Right. She should probably thank him.

"Thank you," she said.

"You're welcome." He released her but stayed quite close to her.

She swallowed. "I, uh, I'm here with my friends, so I'm just going back to..."

"I'm Ray," he said. "And you are...?"

"Rose."

"Nice to meet you, Rose."

His voice was soft. Intimate. Goose bumps broke out on her arms.

"I hope this doesn't seem too strange or forward," he said, "but could I have your number? Maybe we could talk another time, when you're not out with your friends. I don't want to take you away from them now."

"I…sure!" She was slightly discombobulated, as this was unexpected, but it only took a few seconds before she recovered her wits and told him.

She returned to her table with a smile on her face.

"Was that what it looked like?" Amy asked. "You fainted into his arms?"

"I didn't faint," Rose said. "I tripped."

"I'm trying to make it sound more romantic! He asked for your number, didn't he? That's why he took out his phone?"

"Yes."

Amy squealed, and Charlotte gave her a look.

"Did you give him your real number?" Nicole asked. "Or a fake one?"

Rose sat down. "My real number."

But considering what had happened the last time she'd given a guy her number, she told herself not to hope that he'd text her. She'd keep her expectations low so she wouldn't get hurt, and if she didn't hear from him again, she wouldn't take it personally. Wouldn't take it as a sign that she'd be alone forever.

At least, she would try.

She enjoyed being out with her friends more than she had the last time. In the past several months, seeing people had often made her feel more depressed, and then she'd hate herself for not having fun.

Not tonight, though.

She left the cider bar around eleven. It was sad not to be

taking an Uber with Amy or Sierra—Amy had left earlier, and Sierra now lived in the east end with Jake—but Rose told herself it was okay. She wanted her friends to move on with her lives, and Jake seemed like a good guy.

At home, she still felt a little wound up, so she made herself a cup of herbal tea and sat at the kitchen table. She was wasting time on her phone when it vibrated.

Hey, the text read. *It's Ray. Remember me?*

Rose gasped. He'd already texted her!

Of course, she replied.

I know texting you so soon probably isn't the cool thing to do, but I didn't want you to wonder when you'd hear from me.

This was really happening! She stared at the screen, considering how to respond.

You thought I was just waiting around for your text? she asked.

Was that a little flirty, like she'd intended? She started second-guessing herself.

Maybe I hoped you would be.

Ha. I'm very cool and had lots of things to do. She paused her typing and sipped her tea. *Just kidding. I hoped you'd text soon, but I tried not to think about that too much. I've had bad experiences in the past.*

I'm glad you were hoping. And I'm glad you're not one of those Asian women who refuse to date Asian men.

Of course not, she immediately replied. *Are you asking me out on a date?*

She giggled. Who *was* she right now?

Not yet, he texted. *I prefer to get to know people like this first. Maybe I'm a little shy.*

She was slightly disappointed, but only slightly. Perhaps he was right—better to start slowly, rather than what had happened with Cal. She shouldn't have slept with Cal the night she'd met him.

No, she wouldn't shame herself for sex. She'd enjoyed it, but she'd gotten attached to him, and it had made things more complicated—it was okay to admit that, right?

Speaking of Cal...

The front door opened, and Cal walked in. He entered the kitchen and poured himself a glass of water.

"Hey," he said, leaning casually against the counter. "Have a good night?'

"Yeah, I did."

"What'd you do?"

"Just went to the usual cider bar with my friends," she replied.

"A cider bar."

"You more of a beer guy?"

He shrugged, then put down the glass. "Yeah, but I'm flexible."

They weren't having a scintillating conversation, but that was okay. It was nice to have someone to chat with at the end of the day.

She wouldn't tell him about Ray. That would be weird.

Cal washed the glass, put it in the rack, then turned to leave the kitchen.

"Hey, Cal?" she said.

He stopped. "Yeah?"

"I think we'll work out as roommates. You can stay."

He shot her a grin that could melt—

No! What was she thinking?

She should only be having platonic feelings about Cal. She certainly shouldn't be thinking about what had happened last August. They were moving past that, and besides, she had another guy texting her.

"I'm glad," Cal said, that *friendly* grin still on his face. It was nothing more.

He headed upstairs, and Rose had the odd feeling that she'd made a mistake, but that was probably just her brain being weird again.

$$[\ 10 \ ]$$

"I'M FINE," Rose said as she curled up on the couch, phone pressed to her ear.

"Rose," her father said. She wouldn't trade her dad for anyone else's, but occasionally, she wished he were a little less caring and perceptive. "It's Mother's Day. I know it's not the easiest day of the year for you."

Yeah, that was true. It felt like everywhere she looked, she saw Mother's Day greeting cards and bouquets and restaurant specials. Her mother was dead, and the day was further complicated by the fact that her relationship with her mother had been, well, complicated.

In some ways, her mom had been amazing. In other ways, not so much.

It wasn't her mother's mental illness. No, the biggest problem had been Mom's *view* of mental illness. She hadn't really believed that depression was an illness; she saw it as a weakness to be ashamed of. Something to be talked about in hushed voices, if at all; something you should have the strength to overcome in silence.

And she'd absolutely hated that her daughter had it, too.

In her second year of university, Rose had gone to the university health center in desperation, and a doctor had prescribed her some antidepressants. She hadn't thought they were helping, but she'd been told they might take time to work. She'd brought them back to Ottawa when she went home over the Christmas holidays, and she'd been very careful not to let her mother see them. But Mom had done a little snooping, and she'd found them stashed in Rose's desk.

Mom had been *furious*.

Rose recalled saying something about a chemical imbalance in her brain, and her mother had called that bullshit, and then her parents had had a big fight.

Rose hadn't taken antidepressants again until after her mother's death.

She tried not to blame herself for her depression, but it was tough when that was what she'd been brought up to believe. Her mother had been so good about defending her from her grandmother's attacks on her weight, which had started when Rose was seven and chubby. But when it came to depression, Mom hadn't been a supportive parent.

"You know she loved you very much," Dad said, "even if she couldn't always show it. The fact that she ended her life...it doesn't mean she didn't love us."

"I know." Rose didn't understand why he was telling her this; she was very, very aware of what it was like to be suicidal.

"I just..." Dad paused. "I was watching a show the other day, and when one of the characters tried to kill himself, it was implied that he didn't love his family."

Rose sighed. She'd heard such things before.

She shifted on the couch, feeling even more mentally and emotionally exhausted. She'd been sleeping okay recently, and last night hadn't been too bad, but now it was Mother's Day.

"Today isn't a great day," she told her father, "but I think I've been getting better overall. Sometimes the weather helps. One day this week, I'm going to leave the office early and go to Edwards Gardens to see the tulips."

"That sounds nice."

They spoke for a few more minutes, and then Rose made herself a cup of tea and turned on the TV. She had two more episodes left in her rewatch of *The Untamed*, and she snuggled with Fred under a blanket as she started up Netflix. It was warm enough that she didn't actually need a blanket, but it was soothing.

Cal came back an hour later, and rather than just smiling and saying "hey," he took a seat on the recliner.

A little reluctantly, she paused the show.

"What are you watching?" he asked.

"*The Untamed.*"

"What's that?"

"It's a xianxia drama. This is the last of fifty episodes."

He whistled. "Well, I bet you want to know what happens next. I won't—"

"No, no, it's fine," she found herself saying. "This is the third time I've watched it. I know what happens."

"The *third* time?"

"I enjoy rewatching things I like. It's comforting, and I don't have to think too much."

He considered this for a moment and nodded. "Makes sense. Maybe I'll check it out."

She sat up straight. "Really? You're interested?"

"Sure, why not? I keep flipping through Netflix, not sure what to watch. This will keep me busy for a while."

"I'll watch it with you," she offered.

"Yeah? But you're just about finished."

"Like I said, it's comforting for me, and since it's fifty episodes, it's been a while since I saw the first one. Well, only a month, but still. I don't mind at all." She also wanted to make sure this meatloaf, peas-and-carrots white guy, who seemed unfamiliar with Asian dramas, didn't give up after the first episode or two.

"Sure." He actually looked rather pleased about this. And he didn't think she was *too* weird for finishing a show and going right back to the beginning, so that was nice.

"Okay, we'll start this week."

"Sounds good." He paused. "By the way, I got something for you. Well, not *for* you, exactly, but…" He reached into a bag and pulled out a smiling turtle plushie.

A plushie! That certainly wasn't what she'd been expecting.

"It's so cute," she said. "But why are you showing me if it's not for me? You're a big tease." She hoped that sounded appropriately playful but not flirtatious.

"I've noticed that Fred has a bunch of plushie friends who like and comment on his posts. The turtle is going to have her own Instagram account, too."

"Ooh, yes. They can hang out together and we can take pictures of them!" Rose imagined all the fun that Fred and his turtle friend would have, drinking brown sugar boba and similar.

Then the smile slid off her face. She was a little embarrassed about her excitement.

But Cal had bought this turtle, and though she didn't like to think about their one-night stand, he hadn't seemed bothered when he'd given her a teddy bear to hold. Maybe there was no need to feel embarrassed.

Admittedly, the sight of this big bearded guy holding a little turtle was rather adorable. The plushie wasn't tiny, but it looked tiny in his hands.

Dammit, she really needed to stop thinking about his hands. His fingers, which had been inside her. Not just when they were in his bed, but when they were in public.

A man should not look so good holding a stuffed turtle. It was unfair.

She looked away from him.

"Is something wrong?" he asked. "You said you didn't want me to take pictures of you and Fred together, so I thought this would work instead."

"You're not trying to seduce me, are you? Because that ship sailed when…"

She'd been about to reference his lie about his phone being run over, but now she was starting to doubt her conviction that he'd made up that story. This man, who cooked her dinner and wanted to watch *The Untamed* with her, wouldn't have asked for her number if he didn't mean to use it, would he have?

Hmm.

"I know, I know," he said good-naturedly. "Don't worry."

For a moment. she was disappointed, but then she told her brain to stop being silly. Cal was a roommate and friend—she felt comfortable using that word now.

Yes, even though it was Mother's Day, which was far from her favorite day of the year, this weekend had had its good parts, too.

"What should we call your turtle?" she asked.

"Shelly?"

"Because she has a shell?"

Cal scratched the back of his neck. "Uh, yeah, but if you have a better idea…"

"No, I think Shelly is good."

"Great. I'll start her account after I vacuum." He stood up.

Rose returned to the final twenty minutes of *The Untamed* with a smile on her face.

Mother's Day lunch with his family hadn't gone as well as Cal had hoped. He and his siblings had discussed restaurants last week, and Jodi had made a reservation at a nice one.

That had all been fine.

But Dad had been on Cal's case more than usual. Among his

many complaints about Cal's life was the fact that Cal lived with a roommate—apparently, twenty-nine was too old to have a roommate.

Once again, Cal was reminded that at twenty-nine, his parents already had a house and two kids, and his protests about real estate prices in Toronto never seemed to matter to his father. Dad thought the only reason Cal didn't own property was that he was an entitled idiot millennial who didn't know what he was doing with his money.

Which was…sort of true. Anything to do with numbers made him freak out.

But even if he were better with money, it would have been tough for him to buy property, which of course had led to another rant about how Cal should have gone to university.

His attempts to smile and talk about something else hadn't gone well. Nothing had worked until his mother had asked if they could all just get along for once—that was when Dad had given Cal one final glare and focused on his food.

On the way home, Cal had been walking by a store that had a bunch of plushies in the window, and he'd thought of Rose. After the conversation with his father, he'd asked himself whether this was really a good use of his money, then decided that it was. Things that might make his roommate happy were a good use of money. Yes, she'd already said he could stay, but still. He just liked making Rose smile, and she'd been delighted with the turtle.

She'd seemed a little off before that—his guess was something related to Mother's Day. Rose sometimes mentioned her dad, but she never talked about her mom.

Was she not on speaking terms with her mother? Was her mother dead?

He didn't feel like it was his place to ask. If she wanted to tell him, she could, but he wouldn't pry.

He started an Instagram account for Shelly the Turtle, and he followed Fred and a few of the plushies who commented on

Fred's pictures. Then he took a picture of Shelly on his bed and posted it.

Hi, I'm Shelly. I like cake, slow walks in the park, and other turtly things.

He considered changing the "cake" part, but he figured if turtles knew about cake and were able to eat it, they'd like it. Besides, this would give him an excuse to buy a cake.

A little while later, Rose knocked on the door to his room, Fred in hand, and suggested that Fred and Shelly pose in a picture together. She posted the photo to Fred's Instagram with the caption: *This is my new friend Shelly! Our humans live together.* Then she headed back downstairs.

When Penguin Pip commented a few minutes later, asking if their humans were dating, Fred/Rose immediately replied. *No.*

Cal shouldn't feel sad, but he did.

Once again, he couldn't help wondering what would have happened if he hadn't dropped his phone in front of a truck.

[11]

THAT THURSDAY, Cal was putting away the dishes when Rose got home from work. She came into the kitchen, slumped on a chair, and sighed.

"Bad day at work?" he asked.

"Yeah."

"You want to talk about it?" He didn't know what a "bad day at work" looked like for an engineer, but he could listen, even if he wouldn't understand.

"The client for this project wants a whole bunch of changes and…" She shook her head. "Nah, I don't really want to talk about it."

She was wearing a pink blouse that he'd seen her wear once before. Not that he was trying to keep track of her work clothes, but he couldn't help noticing. He liked the shirt on her, but then again, he liked a lot of things on her.

Just then, her stomach gurgled. Her eyes widened, and she looked embarrassed.

"How about I make you something for dinner?" he said.

"That's really not necessary. I can figure out my own food." But she sounded overwhelmed at the thought.

"I was just going to heat up some leftover chili—there's enough for you—and make a salad. Nothing fancy."

"If you're sure…"

"Of course. Then maybe we can start *The Untamed*."

Her eyes lit up. "Yeah? Oh, you're going to love it so much. I hope."

She went upstairs to change, and when she came back downstairs, she was wearing a T-shirt in the same shade of pink as her blouse. It pulled tightly against her breasts, and he swallowed hard and nearly sliced his finger instead of the tomato. She was also wearing stretchy yoga pants, and he wouldn't comment on how good her ass looked in those.

"Is something wrong?" she asked.

"No, no," he said. "I'll be done in, uh, five minutes."

Soon, they were sitting in front of the TV with their chili and salad. The show started, and Cal was more than a little confused. Not because of the subtitles—though he didn't often watch shows with subtitles, it didn't take long to get used to that. Still, he wasn't sure what was going on, and he couldn't tell all the characters apart.

They got to the end of the episode.

"Shall we watch another one?" she asked. She'd been sitting up on the couch to eat earlier, but now she was lying down, her head propped up on throw pillows, and she was covered by a blanket. He, meanwhile, was in the recliner.

"Sure." He really wanted to figure out what the hell was going on.

But at the end of the second episode, he was still confused, yet he wanted to keep watching—and not only so he could spend time with Rose.

They watched one more episode.

"So, what do you think?" she asked.

"I, uh…it's good."

"You're not sure what's happening, right?"

"Yes," he said, relieved he hadn't had to say it himself.

"Don't worry. The first time I saw it, it took several episodes before I felt like I had a handle on things."

"And I can't tell everyone apart." He wasn't sure he was supposed to admit that. It was bad to be a white guy saying he couldn't tell a bunch of Asian people apart, right? But there were lots of characters, and they all had similar hairstyles.

"Me, too," she said. "I mean, I can now, but I struggled with it a little the first time. If you need me to confirm who someone is, just ask, but I'm not going to explain the whole plot—you'll figure it out as we watch more. But isn't it still awesome, even if you're confused?"

"Yeah," he said with a laugh, "it kind of is. Just one more question: what's cultivating?"

He didn't fully understand her explanation, but that was okay. He could look it up later. Part of the problem was that he kept being distracted by the animated way she talked, so different from how she'd looked when she'd gotten home from work. It was hard not to smile around her.

Too bad she still thought he was a liar who'd never planned to text her. Nothing was gonna happen, even if, at times, it felt like they were a couple living together. Or maybe that was just because it had been a while since he'd had a roommate, and he'd never had a female roommate before.

Yeah, he shouldn't think about it too much.

Rose stared out her bedroom window as Cal cut the grass in the backyard.

Living with him had certainly been going better than she'd feared. At first, she'd figured he was on his best behavior so she didn't ask him to find somewhere else to live, but in the weeks since she'd agreed he could stay, not much had changed. He continued to do his chores and keep common areas fairly neat, and occasionally he cooked for her, too.

She, of course, returned the favor. She'd asked if he liked fish, and when he'd responded that he did, she'd made steamed fish for him, along with rice and bok choy. She'd been a little afraid of how the meal would be received, but he'd contentedly scarfed down a large portion. The man could sure put away a lot of food. He had a physical job, so she supposed it made sense.

She'd also introduced him to Turtle Chips—the sweet corn ones were her favorite—and suggested he take a picture of Shelly with the bag. It turned out Cal quite liked the taste, too, though he'd been momentarily confused, thinking they were actually made of turtle.

When her phone vibrated, she looked at the comment from Penguin Pip.

Gee, Fred, it seems like your human and Shelly's human have been spending lots of time together.

Fred/Rose didn't immediately reply.

Yeah, they'd been spending some time together, most of it watching *The Untamed*—they'd now seen twenty episodes. She could imagine them living together for a while, and he made her feel…cared for. Like when he volunteered to cook for her on the days when she needed it most. Nothing fancy, and he always spoke as though it was no big deal, but still.

She did her best to keep the worst of her depression from him; she certainly didn't tell him everything that was going through her mind. No, she'd just say, "Let's watch *The Untamed* tonight." Somehow, watching it with him was extra comforting.

The sound of the lawnmower stopped, and Cal walked over to the fence to talk to the older women who lived next door. One of them held up their small dog, Beast, and Cal scratched behind her ears. Beast looked enamored with him.

I understand, Beast.

No! What was wrong with her? Rose certainly wasn't *enam-*

ored with Cal. He was just a nice guy and a good roommate, though he did look quite attractive when he was petting a small dog…and also when he returned to cutting the grass. Maybe she should go downstairs so she could get a better view of his arms.

No!

It would be a bad idea to slobber over her roommate. Not that she'd be slobbering over him, exactly, though on occasion, she found it tough to ignore that he really was a good-looking man.

But she *could* use some tea, so she walked downstairs and started boiling water in the electric kettle.

Unfortunately, Cal chose that exact moment to come inside. It was a warm day for May, and his skin was glistening with sweat. He lifted up the bottom of his shirt to wipe off his face…

Goddammit!

Alas, she didn't manage to hide her stunned look.

"Sorry," he said, dropping his shirt.

No, no. That wasn't what she wanted him to do. This was making her all mixed up.

"It's okay," she said. "I don't mind. In fact, I've been meaning to ask…would you mind if I occasionally go without a bra downstairs? They're not always the most comfortable, and after work…"

Oh, God. Occasionally, it seemed like the connection between her brain and mouth was broken. Like the time last summer when she'd made that comment about her stuffed alpaca at Nautilus. And now she was thinking more about that night, the way he'd pressed her against the wall and slid his fingers inside her, while she could still hear traffic and the noises from the patio, just steps away.

Apparently, her brain was broken, too. Those thoughts needed to stop.

"But I won't if it makes *you* uncomfortable," she continued.

"I don't mind," he said stiffly, which wasn't like him. "Stiff" wasn't a word she'd use to describe Cal, unless…

Stop it, brain!

"Are you sure?" she asked. "I don't want you to feel pressured."

"Trust me, I don't feel pressured," he said, though his voice sounded slightly strained.

He headed upstairs—she couldn't blame him for leaving this awkward situation—just as the water started to boil. She decided that a whole pot of jasmine tea was in order today. She had a lovely teapot with plum blossoms that made her smile whenever she used it.

Maybe she could read now. Yeah. That was a good idea. A pot of tea and a book she'd read before. That would be a good way to calm her brain—and body.

Instead, she ended up wasting time on her phone for fifteen minutes, and she was about to finally set her phone aside when it vibrated.

Ooh, it was Ray.

They'd been texting on and off for the past few weeks. Nothing much, just giving each other recs for Asian movies and such. But now he was saying that he couldn't wait any longer to see her, and how would she like to go out for dinner next Saturday?

Rose nearly squealed, but there was a hollow sensation in her chest.

Why wasn't she completely happy about this? Wasn't it what she wanted?

Why was her brain being all weird today?

She'd thought the heaviness of her depression was easing, but this seemed like a sign that it wasn't. Though she shouldn't get angry at herself for not being thrilled, she couldn't seem to help it. She really ought to be happy. She and Ray had had the sort of meeting that would make a good story for their kids some day.

No, not kids. Nieces and nephews.

But what if Ray wanted kids? When should she ask him? She was thirty-five, so maybe it made sense to talk about this near the beginning. Dating was different at this age, so she'd heard, but it wasn't like she'd done much dating in her twenties. She'd had other things to deal with, and the few times she'd gone out with someone, it hadn't led to anything lasting.

She sighed and turned on the TV in the living room just as Cal came downstairs, grabbed a can of pop, and sat in the recliner.

"Mind if I watch something?" she asked. She could go upstairs, but—

"Sure," he said, "as long as you're not watching *The Untamed* without me."

"I would never do that." She laughed, already feeling a bit better. "Hey, Cal?"

"Yeah?"

"I believe that your phone got run over by a truck. I'm sorry I didn't at first."

"No big deal." He looked at her for a moment, his gaze more intense than usual, as if to say, *Does that mean you want to start things up again?*

Then it was gone, and she wondered if she'd imagined it.

Besides, it didn't matter. They were roommates; it was too dangerous to hook up again. Plus, she'd spent so many months pissed at him, and she still wasn't entirely over how he'd made her feel—not that her feelings were all his fault, of course.

"I'm glad you're my roommate," she said.

Roommate. Nothing more.

[12]

C AL RARELY GOT angry at himself. He was used to his occasional stupid behavior. It was just a fact of life, so what point was there in being angry?

But that Thursday, he was walking up to the house when a delivery person arrived with a vase of red roses.

Yep, someone was sending his roommate roses, and he didn't like it.

As Cal set the vase of roses on the kitchen table, he remembered that different colored roses had different meanings—and weren't red ones the most romantic?

His hand curled into a fist.

If he hadn't been the doofus who'd had his phone run over by a truck—a feat so ridiculous that Rose hadn't believed him until recently—he could be the one sending her roses instead.

Even if they were getting along well as roommates, she'd made it clear that his chance had passed. So Cal didn't let on that he kept thinking about the night they'd met, nor that he wanted to make her smile as much possible.

Usually, he'd just shrug it off and move on—there were lots of other women out there—but faced with these red roses, he was finding it particularly difficult.

He was…jealous? Was that the name for this feeling?

Huh.

He wasn't used to feeling jealous. It was strange.

After having a shower and putting on some fresh clothes, he headed back downstairs, and he was debating what to have for dinner when he heard a key in the front door.

"You got a delivery," he called out.

Rose bounded into the kitchen. "Ray told me he was going to send me something… Oh my God! He sent me flowers." She leaned over, closed her eyes, and took a deep sniff. An expression of delight crossed her face.

It wasn't that Cal hated the idea of anyone but him putting that look on her face. If a night out with her friends made her happy, he was all for it. But this guy was clearly something other than a friend.

"Are you seeing someone?" Cal asked, trying to sound like his usual casual self.

"I guess?" she said. "We met a few weeks ago. I tripped on my feet, and Ray caught me and asked for my number. We've been texting, and we're finally going on a date this Saturday."

But from the sounds of it, Ray hadn't slept with her, hadn't licked her until she screamed, and nothing could change the fact that Cal had apparently been the first person to do that to her.

"Cal?" Rose said. "You okay?"

"Yeah, yeah. Of course I am. I hope you enjoy your date." It was difficult to tell such an enormous lie.

Rose shot him an odd look, but then she grabbed the vase off the table and headed to the staircase. "We'll watch a few episodes later, okay?"

She skipped up the steps, and Cal was thankful that she was taking the roses to her bedroom. He didn't want to see them sitting on the kitchen table for the next few days. This Ray guy was probably better suited to her than Cal, and he likely didn't get his phones run over by trucks.

Cal hated the bastard.

Yep, he could use a night out this weekend. Get his mind off the situation. He texted Marv, and a few minutes later, he noticed that Rose had posted a picture of Fred sniffing the flowers.

Hmph.

Time for a beer.

Rose twirled in front of the mirror. She thought she looked pretty good in this black dress, a purchase from a recent shopping trip with Nicole.

It was the sort of dress her mother might have picked out with her, back in the day. She'd enjoyed shopping with her mom.

Rose had never been thin, unlike her parents and brothers, but Mom had never made her feel like that was a problem, and she was always trying to find flattering clothes for Rose. When they went to a store and couldn't find anything nice, Mom would complain about the retailer's sizing and styles, never about Rose's rather apple-shaped body.

And when Po Po criticized Rose's weight, Mom fought back. When Rose faked a headache and didn't want to go to Po Po's for dinner, Mom hadn't pushed her.

With another mother, Rose might have developed a fucked-up relationship with food, but she'd been lucky. Sure, she sometimes wished she looked different, but in general, she was fine with her body—and she thought she looked hot tonight. Ray hadn't told her exactly where they were going, but he was taking her out for dinner. They planned to meet at a subway station near the restaurant.

Rose was humming and touching up her makeup when her phone buzzed. She read the text from Ray.

I'm so sorry...family emergency...

The words swam in front of her face and tears came to her eyes. One canceled date, and he had a good excuse—she shouldn't cry. No, she should be worried for Ray. She knew what a family emergency could look like; she knew all too well.

It's okay, she texted. *I understand.*

She ought to say more, but for some reason, the words weren't coming.

It was rare for her to have a date, and she'd been looking forward to it all week. As it turned out, she'd been excited for nothing. She was pissed at herself for being so disappointed when she knew they could reschedule and her concerns should be for Ray and his family.

Dammit, why was she like this? Was she too unstable to date at all?

She tugged off her dress, threw it on the bed, and put on her pajamas before heading downstairs, where Cal was tying his shoelaces.

"I thought you had a date?" he said.

"I was supposed to." She tried not to sound morose. "But he had some kind of emergency, so I'm going to...I don't know. Eat ramen and watch a movie, maybe."

No big deal, right? But sometimes, when a whole night of being alone stretched in front of her, it was a little scary.

Chin up, Rose. She and Fred would find a nice movie, and sure, it seemed a little pathetic to spend the evening with her stuffed alpaca, but it was okay! There was nothing wrong with her.

At the thought of all the positive self-talk she'd have to do to keep herself from spiraling downward, she already felt exhausted. She could do it. It was just...yeah.

"What are you up to?" she asked Cal.

"Meeting some friends at the pub," he said. "You want to come?"

"Oh! I wasn't asking because I wanted you to invite me. I was just trying to be friendly…I didn't mean…"

He chuckled. "Rose, I didn't think you meant it like that, but you're welcome to come with me."

"I wouldn't want to intrude."

"It's just a bunch of people drinking beer, watching baseball, and playing pool, maybe. Nothing formal."

The idea of spending time with people she didn't know was a bit alarming. It might take a lot out of her, but she really didn't want to stay home.

"Well…"

"Aw, come on," he said. "It'll be a good time."

He was talking as though it was no big deal, and maybe for him, that was true. But Rose was often incapable of relaxing, no matter how much she tried. Or maybe the fact that she was *trying* was the problem, but if she didn't…

"Does anyone know about us?" she blurted out. "I mean, do your friends know that your roommate is also your one-night stand from last August?"

"Only Marv knows. I'll text him and tell him not to say anything."

"Okay. Cool. I guess I'll come. Just give me five minutes to get changed, alright?"

Rose headed upstairs to put on jeans and a T-shirt. She decided to go full casual and wear running shoes rather than the heels she would have worn for the date.

The pub turned out to be within walking distance. Fairly close to Nautilus, in fact. It was a generic sort of pub that you could find all over the city—not a place you went to for the amazing food or amazing drinks, but for the company.

When they stepped inside, Cal approached a table with a white guy and a South Asian woman. She was wearing a Jays jersey, and they were both half watching the baseball game on TV as they drank their beer.

"Yo, Cal." The guy stood up, and he and Cal gave each other a back-slapping hug.

"I didn't know you were bringing someone tonight," the woman said to Cal.

"This is Rose, my housemate. Rose, meet Meena and Levi."

There were a bunch of murmured nice-to-meet-yous, then Rose busied herself with looking at the menu. Once the waitress came around to take their orders, Cal's attention was drawn away by a guy he knew from work—Peter—who was sitting a few tables down.

Levi turned to Rose. "How's living with Cal? You didn't know each other beforehand, right?"

"We didn't," Rose lied, "but it's been going well. He's a good roommate."

"And he brought you out tonight," Meena said, perhaps sounding a little suspicious that there was something going on between them.

"Oh, that's just because I was supposed to go on a date," Rose said breezily, as if dates were regular occurrences for her, "but he canceled at the last minute and I had no plans tonight."

"This guy canceled on you?"

"Family emergency, so here I am." Her voice sounded a little weird. She wasn't used to meeting new people, and she really wanted them to like her, even if she wasn't meeting them as Cal's girlfriend.

Whoa. Why was the phrase "Cal's girlfriend" on her mind?

The waitress brought over their drinks. Rose's lager was perfectly drinkable. Not the kind of thing she'd go out of her way to have, but it would do.

Cal returned and sat down next to her. "When you want to go, let me know and we'll head out."

"Don't worry about me," she said. "Stay as long as you like. I'll be safe walking home."

"Might as well walk with you, since we live together."

"If you're sure." Rose looked around the table. "Where did you all meet?"

"High school," Levi said.

"What was Cal like in high school?"

"He was super emo," Meena said. "Dyed his hair black and… Hey, Cal, what are you doing with my drink?"

"Just keeping it safe until you talk about something more appropriate."

"Wait, are you serious?" Rose asked Meena.

"No, no, I'm kidding of course. Here, I'll show you a picture."

Meena pulled out her phone and it took her a surprisingly short time to come up with a picture of Cal, his body a little smaller, his hair a lot shorter.

"We were theater geeks," Meena said.

"You were?" Rose looked at Cal, wide-eyed. She hadn't expected that.

He shrugged. "Yeah, I was mostly backstage."

A Black guy with glasses showed up a few minutes later. He was introduced to Rose as Damien, and he immediately started talking up Cal, until Cal said, "Hey, man, she's my friend. I'm not trying to get laid."

A few moments later, when no one was looking, Cal turned to Rose and winked.

She couldn't stop her face from heating, and she chugged some beer to cool herself off. What exactly did he mean by that wink? He was just playing around, right?

Yet as the evening continued, she couldn't help but be reminded of the night they'd met, all those months ago. Something about being out at a bar, she supposed, even if this place didn't have murals of kraken.

What would have happened if they'd gone on that date? Would they be together now? Would she have met his friends last year?

Or would it still have ended in heartbreak?

"Hey, you okay?" Cal leaned closer to her, and his nearness made her momentarily disoriented.

"Yeah, I'm good," she said at last.

"Sad about being stuck with me rather than on a date?"

Yes, that was right. She should be thinking about Ray, not Cal.

"I'm managing," she said.

When Marv and his girlfriend finally arrived, Rose had a little trouble looking at Marv, knowing that he was aware of what had happened between her and Cal. But he didn't say anything, as Cal had promised.

However, when she came back from the washroom a little while later, she noticed that Marv and Cal had their heads bent together, talking separately from the rest of the group. She couldn't help wondering if they were talking about her history with Cal, but when she sat down beside him, she realized it had something to do with baseball.

"Not a baseball fan?" Meena asked.

"Uh, no," Rose said. "Not really."

"That's okay. We don't have to talk about the sport. Just which players you think are cute."

At that moment, Cal and Marv's conversation became a little more animated, and Cal knocked his half-full pint off the table with his elbow. Rose leapt out of the way before it could soak her; only a few drops splashed on her jeans before the glass fell to the ground and smashed.

"Aw, hell," Cal said, without much annoyance behind his words.

For some reason, Rose couldn't help remembering the time she'd broken an empty mug back in the winter. She'd burst into tears. Not a normal reaction for her, but the thought of having to clean it up had been overwhelming.

Cal found the waitress, apologized for the mess, and handed some napkins to Rose.

"It's okay, I barely got wet," she said.

Oh, no. Now that word was making her think of…other things.

She pushed those thoughts out of her mind and concentrated on talking to Cal's friends.

It was a decent night out. She didn't have a wonderfully amazing time, no, but it was enjoyable enough, and much better than trying to figure out how to spend the evening alone without getting too sad. Cal was attentive, making sure she was included in the conversation and had enough to drink. She didn't have too much of an appetite, but he ordered the table some nachos, and she enjoyed a few of those.

At eleven thirty, she told him she was ready to head out. As they walked home together, she was reminded, once again, of that night back in August—that was the last time she'd been out after dark with him. They'd headed back to his place together…

And now, his place was her place.

She opened the door, and as she untied her shoes, she said, "Thanks for inviting me out tonight. I appreciate it. It was just what I needed."

She'd never been very good with canceled plans. She had to mentally prepare herself for social occasions, and when they didn't happen, it was a letdown.

Her shoes off, she stood up, and Cal was…closer than she'd expected him to be. Only a few inches separated her head from his chest, and when her gaze darted to the side, it landed on his biceps. She couldn't help wanting to grab them.

"Thank you," she said again, to stop herself from saying any of the thoughts floating around in her mind.

He shrugged. "No big deal. Glad you could come out with us. I mean, I'm not glad your plans were canceled, but…"

She'd always been envious of people like Cal. Ones who could just shrug and move on, who could go with the flow.

She took a step but tripped on his foot. He caught her, holding onto her for a few seconds so she could find her balance, but even once her feet were solidly planted on the floor, she was off-balance. He was so close, and once upon a time, he'd made her feel things that nobody else had.

She nearly asked how seeing those red roses from Ray had made him feel, but thankfully, she hadn't lost complete control over her mouth.

It was silly to think there was a chance that Cal would have been jealous…right?

It was silly to want that.

Sure, he might have intended to call her back in the summer, but he was the sort of guy who'd move on without a problem. She doubted he was thinking of kissing her now, whereas she was thinking of tilting her head up and…

Holy shit! She was thinking of kissing her roommate.

Bad idea, brain. Bad idea.

"Goodnight!" she called as she hurried upstairs.

In her bedroom, she closed the door and sank to the floor, wondering what might have happened if his phone hadn't been run over by a fucking truck.

No, she shouldn't. She should leave the past in the past.

She walked over to the roses on her desk and gave them a sniff.

[13]

"Is this okay?" Ray asked, gesturing to a restaurant. Its sign proclaimed that it specialized in Hakka cuisine.

"Of course," Rose said with a smile on her face, but inside, she was oddly disappointed.

It made zero sense. She'd never been to a Hakka restaurant before, and she wanted to try it. But apparently, she wished Ray had chosen a restaurant that wasn't what she wanted.

Why?

She liked this guy. She wanted a relationship.

If only her brain were more logical.

He smiled at her over his shoulder, and something about that smile seemed a little…off.

Why was she thinking that? Perhaps she shouldn't trust herself. Her thinking could be flawed due to her mental illness. If she was weirded out by his smile, it was probably her brain trying to find reasons for this not to work out because some part of her believed she didn't deserve it.

But she did deserve it, dammit.

Ray was a nice guy who'd brought her to a restaurant she

wanted to try. He was a lawyer, and he had a large family, all of whom lived in the Toronto area.

The two of them were shown to their table, and they studied the menu together. He suggested the chili chicken, and she picked a noodle dish.

After the waiter came to take their order and they no longer had the menu to discuss, there was silence.

"Sorry," she said. "I haven't been on a date in a while."

"Me, neither." He paused as he poured some tea. "I have a profile on a few dating sites, but you know Asian men often don't fare well on those."

She nodded. "You ought to do well, though. You have a good job, and you're…" She gestured toward him.

"I'm what, Rose?" he asked with a wiggle of his eyebrows.

"You're very handsome."

"Is that so?"

"And romantic. The flowers were lovely."

"I'm glad you liked them."

Rose opened her mouth, about to tell him how she'd taken pictures of Fred with the roses. But then she'd have to explain her stuffed alpaca, and that probably wasn't the best thing to do on a first date.

Damn, this dating business was complicated. If only she'd been like Charlotte and decided to get some "dating practice" first, then conveniently fallen in love with her dating-practice partner. In fact, those love lessons had been Rose's idea, inspired by a book she'd read, but she'd never tried it herself.

"I hope your family is okay?" she said instead, remembering why Ray had canceled last time.

"Yeah. My dad fell off a ladder."

"Oh no!"

"He's fine now. My mom just freaked me out on the phone, making it sound worse than it actually was. You know how moms are."

She murmured her agreement, not wanting to bring up the fact that she didn't have a mom anymore.

The food arrived, and they busied themselves with filling their plates. It was all delicious, especially the chili chicken.

Although Rose was enjoying herself well enough, she didn't understand why she wasn't enjoying herself more. Maybe her brain was getting in the way again, or this could just be what happened when you didn't date much. Once she'd gone on a few more dates with Ray, she wouldn't have to tell herself how she ought to be feeling or overthink every word.

Yes, it was all going fine.

After dinner, they went to a cute little café and shared a slice of cake, then he walked her back to the subway station. He looked at her in a way she couldn't quite interpret. Expectantly, as though she was supposed to invite him home with her after the first date?

No, she was probably imagining it.

"I had a great time tonight," she said.

"Next weekend, can I take you out again?" he asked.

"I'll be visiting my family in Ottawa, but we could do something this coming week?"

"I'd love to. Unfortunately, I have a really big case at work."

They agreed to meet up on the Thursday after she returned from Ottawa. Then he leaned forward and pressed a kiss to her lips, deepening it as soon as she started kissing him back. It was a pleasant kiss, though she couldn't help wishing he had a short beard that would scrape against her skin.

That didn't mean she was thinking of Cal. Of course not. She was just thinking about...a stranger with a beard. Yes. That was all.

She said goodbye to Ray and headed home, totally unprepared for what she found there.

~

Cal was attempting to bake cookies.

He had basic cooking skills, but not much in the way of baking skills. He'd helped people bake before, but he'd never selected the recipe and been in charge of everything himself. At his old apartment, Mrs. Weissman used to bake for him on a regular basis, and he'd never felt the need to do so.

However, earlier that evening, he'd decided homemade peanut butter cookies were a good idea—Rose had mentioned them, offhand, the other day—and he'd gone to the store to get a few ingredients. He didn't have an electric mixer, but she'd said he could use her kitchen stuff as needed, and he was (somewhat) confident that he wouldn't break her mixer.

Everything had been going well until he'd gone to take the cookies out of the oven after ten minutes, as the recipe said. They were supposed to be "golden brown," but Cal was unclear on exactly what that meant. Since the cookies contained peanut butter, weren't they sort of golden brown to start with?

He'd thought they'd seemed a little underdone, so he'd left them in for another two minutes before taking them out, feeling rather proud of himself. He'd made a batch of cookies.

That pride had disappeared once he'd actually tried one of the cookies. Something wasn't right, and he'd had no idea what to do. He'd decided the best thing would be to start over again and be very careful to follow the recipe.

They'd turned out exactly the same as the first time.

After fifteen minutes of puzzling, he'd happened on the idea that the cookies weren't baked enough, which led to a frenzy of googling.

Is it safe to eat uncooked flour?

Is it safe to eat uncooked eggs?

Is it safe to eat uncooked peanut butter?

Yes, he was aware that last question was stupid, but he'd pressed "search" before realizing he ate peanut butter on toast all the time.

When Rose arrived home and walked into the kitchen, he still didn't know exactly where he'd gone wrong.

"How was your date?" he asked casually, trying to pretend that the catastrophic mess wasn't entirely his fault. To his relief, she was alone.

"It was good," she replied.

He admired her in that black dress for a moment before saying, "You going to see him again?" As though it was no big deal to him either way.

"Yep."

She didn't seem as excited as he'd thought she might be. He refrained from pumping his fist—it wasn't like he was pleased she wasn't excited…right?

"What were you doing in here?" she asked.

Well, you see, Rose, I had this vision of feeding you homemade peanut butter cookies and tea after your date because it would make you smile, especially if I took a picture of Shelly munching on a cookie.

Instead, he said, "Figured I'd try to make peanut butter cookies, but they didn't work out. So I tried again, and they still didn't work out. Don't worry, I'll clean up the kitchen."

She tapped her chin. "Hmm. Let me see the recipe."

He handed over his phone, and her mouth parted in an "O."

Dammit, he'd done something silly, hadn't he?

"Cal," she said, "what temperature did you set the oven at?"

"One seventy-five. Just like the recipe said."

It had seemed a little low to him—meatloaf, for example, he cooked at three-fifty—but what did he know about baking?

Rose walked over to the oven and pointed to a spot on the temperature dial. "Here?"

He nodded.

"The recipe you're using is from the UK," she said. "The temperature is given in Celsius, but this oven is in Fahrenheit. You see the smaller numbers? Those are Celsius."

This wasn't making a whole lot of sense to him. He vaguely

remembered there being different types of temperature units, but he'd thought that only applied to weather.

But of course, it could apply to ovens, too.

She laughed, but he didn't feel like she was laughing *at* him. Or judging him.

"I'll turn the oven back on, to a higher temperature." She turned the dial. "In a few minutes, we'll pop the ones on the tray back in the oven. Not sure exactly how long they'll have to bake, but I suspect they'll still turn out okay, assuming you didn't also mix up sugar and salt."

"Nah, I just made the one mistake." At least, that was what he hoped.

"I'll be right back. Gonna get changed."

When she returned a few minutes later, she was wearing pajama pants and a big T-shirt. He was pretty sure she had no bra on underneath, which he'd said was fine, but now... God, he really had to stop thinking about her breasts and the time he'd gotten to touch them.

"You okay?" she asked.

"Yeah." *Just trying not to picture you naked.*

Rose decided the cookies were now "golden brown," and he didn't question her judgment. She seemed to have a better idea of what was going on here than he did. He turned on the kettle for tea, since he'd noticed she drank lots of tea.

A few minutes later, they worked as a team to put the cookies onto the racks, and she placed the last one on a plate.

"I assume I get to eat one?" she asked.

"Of course. It wasn't like I planned to eat them all myself."

Though he could have. He was impressed with how well they'd turned out. They weren't quite as good as Mrs. Weissman's peanut butter cookies, but that was an impossible standard. Considering that twenty minutes ago, he had no idea what the hell was going on, he was pretty pleased.

And Rose hadn't called him an idiot, even though he couldn't imagine she'd make a mistake like that in the first place.

She poured him some herbal tea from the teapot, then smiled at him in a way that was utterly perfect, and he was overcome with an urge to kiss her. Just like last weekend, when they'd come back from the pub together and she'd tripped over his foot.

But she'd gone on a date with another guy tonight. For all Cal knew, she could have been kissing this Ray guy not half an hour ago.

She glanced at the clock on the wall. "It's not too late yet. What do you say we watch another episode or two of *The Untamed?*"

"Sounds good to me," he said.

Eating cookies and drinking tea out of tiny-ass tea cups with Rose?

Yup, sounded pretty perfect to him.

She turned on the TV, and he brought out her tea and a couple more cookies.

"Thanks," she said cheerily. She snuggled up on the couch with her sloth.

For the first time in his life, Cal found himself jealous of a stuffed sloth. Yup, it wasn't enough that he was jealous of the guy she'd gone on a date with tonight; he was jealous of a damn toy.

He remembered, from their long-ago night together, that when she went to bed, she liked to hold a stuffed animal—he'd volunteered himself, and she'd said that wouldn't be the same. But maybe, when she was snuggling something when she was awake, she'd prefer a human.

He didn't ask, though.

They ended up watching three episodes and eating more than three cookies each, and even if he didn't get to put his arm around her, it was still a pretty good night.

[14]

"Lou," Rose said.

Her brother made some noises but didn't wake up. His head bobbed in a way that looked rather painful.

Dad chuckled. He stood up from the recliner and rested his hand on Lou's shoulder.

"Imitate the sound of a baby crying," Rose suggested. "That'll wake him."

Instead, Dad shook Lou's shoulder.

Lou finally opened his eyes, looking disoriented. "What's going on? Are they awake?"

"Not that I know of," Dad said, patting Lou's cheek. "Go up to bed."

"How long was I asleep on the chair?"

"Twenty minutes," Rose said.

Lou's wife had put the twins to bed a while ago, but he'd said he would stay up since Rose was visiting. He hadn't been conscious for long, though. He mumbled some goodnights, then headed upstairs.

Now it was just Rose and her father. She was sitting on the futon that she'd slept on last night and would sleep on again tonight. It was the first time she'd visited Ottawa since her father had moved in with Lou's family. The first time since he'd sold the old house. She could no longer sleep in her childhood bedroom when she came to Ottawa, and that was totally fine. She was glad her father had retired and wasn't living alone, though she did miss it.

"How are you feeling?" Dad asked.

Rose smiled at him. His hair was completely white now, and his glasses were slightly askew. Was he losing weight, or was she just worrying needlessly?

"I'm okay."

He studied her, as if trying to figure out whether she was telling the truth. "Are you happy living in Toronto? Are you sure you don't want to move back here?"

It was the first time he'd ever asked her that.

A year after her mom's death, Rose had decided she couldn't stand to live in Ottawa anymore. She needed a change. She'd felt guilty about leaving her father, but he'd told her it was fine. She'd started looking for jobs in Toronto and had been lucky to find one relatively quickly.

"Yeah," she said, "I'm sure."

"It's not because I'm too demanding and in-your-face and you think you wouldn't get a moment's peace if we lived in the same city again?"

He was making a joke, wasn't he?

"You know that's not true," she assured him, just in case.

She really couldn't have asked for a better father. She'd told him that before, because they weren't the kind of family who never spoke about feelings—at least not anymore.

Still, it didn't mean they talked about everything.

Sometimes when they spoke, she could feel her mom's presence so strongly. Other times, she was acutely aware of her mother's absence, of what would have been said if her mother were there, too.

"Lou and Tracey don't expect you to get up with the twins at night, do they?" she asked.

"Never," Dad said. "But it's nice for her to have a second person around during the day, especially with two babies."

Rose suspected many women would find it a pain in the ass to have their father-in-law around all the time, but her dad would be helpful and not intrusive. He wouldn't question every parenting decision Lou and Tracey made.

Rose's phone buzzed, and she didn't look at it. However, when it buzzed again, her dad said, "You should get it."

She took a quick look. The text was from Ray, saying he hoped she was having a good time with her family and he wished he could have seen her tonight. She smiled and set her phone aside.

"Is it a boy?" her dad asked.

"He's not a boy. He's..." Well, she didn't know how old Ray was, actually, but he was about her age.

"And you're dating?"

"We've been on one date, yes."

Dad waited a beat. "I assume you aren't willing to share details about him yet?"

"You assume correctly."

He stood up and patted her head when he said goodnight to her—she'd always be his baby. Then he headed down the hall to his room at the far end of the main floor.

He wasn't moving more slowly than usual, was he?

She was just paranoid.

She looked at her phone again.

I miss you, Ray had texted.

She stared at the words. They'd only had one date, so wasn't it a little soon to miss each other?

I'm excited for Thursday! she replied.

She hadn't wanted to say *Miss you too*, but maybe he would read into the fact that she hadn't responded with those words?

It was rather thrilling to have a guy who took her on dates and texted her like this, but Rose wanted to get to the point where they snuggled up together on Sunday mornings and knew they could count on each other. She wanted companionship.

Wait. Was it weird that she wasn't looking forward to sex? That she wasn't thinking of sleeping with Ray yet? The kiss had been pleasant, and she'd like to do that again, but she couldn't imagine inviting him in after the next date.

Yet Cal had had his fingers inside her not long after they'd met...

She figured her body was just trying to protect her now, after what had happened with Cal. Sex could never be entirely meaningless to Rose, and Cal's apparent rejection of her had probably hurt all the more because they'd gone to bed together.

Yes, that must be it; it didn't mean she wasn't attracted to Ray.

Her phone buzzed again, but this time, it was Cal.

Or Shelly, rather.

Cal had made a speech bubble out of white paper and marker that said "I miss you, Fred," and he'd taken a picture of Shelly lying on a pillow, the speech bubble coming out of her mouth. Rose couldn't help laughing in delight.

Shelly doesn't look all that sad, Rose texted. *She's still smiling.*

That might look like a smile to you, but it's not. I'm the expert on Shelly.

Rose tiptoed around the house, as though she was doing something illicit in her brother's home, rather than simply looking for a marker and paper. Eventually, she managed to locate the necessary supplies, and she grinned as she wrote a speech bubble for Fred, who'd accompanied her to Ottawa.

"O Shelly. How I miss thee."

Rather than texting it to Cal, Rose posted it on Instagram. She was too proud of her handiwork not to have more than one person—and a plush turtle—see it.

Penguin Pip commented a few minutes later. *Have you been reading Shakespeare?*

Merry Lamb: *Do you have romantic feelings for Shelly, Fred?*

Fred the Alpaca: *The platonic love I have for Shelly runs deep.*

Penguin Pip: *I'm with Merry. I think it's a budding romance!*

Rose started feeling defensive. She and Cal were roommates and friends. There was nothing romantic...

Wait a second. This conversation was about Fred and Shelly, not Rose and Cal. Why was she getting confused?

Merry Lamb: *But they're in denial.*

Penguin Pip: *The course of true love never did run smooth.*

Merry Lamb: *Are your humans in love, Fred?*

Fred the Alpaca: *No*

Penguin Pip: *Hmm...*

Shelly the Turtle: *Really, they're not.*

Fabulous the Unicorn: *But wouldn't it be FABULOUS if they were?*

Rose thought about that for a second. Cal understood her, and he was good to her. She already knew they could live together, since they'd been doing it for over a month now, which was a decent start.

She also knew the sex would be excellent since, well, they'd slept together last year, and she'd be lying if she said she never thought about it. Those meaty arms wrapped around her, his beard scraping her inner thighs, his fingers sliding through her wetness...

The cry of one of the twins upstairs—quickly followed by the cry of the other—interrupted her sexual thoughts, but she kept thinking about Cal.

Cal, who'd tried to bake cookies at 175°F instead of 175°C.

Cal, who'd made her meatloaf.

Cal, who'd bought himself a plush turtle that was currently conversing with her plush alpaca on Instagram.

No, it seemed too risky. This guy had already broken her

heart once, and he was her roommate, for God's sake. If things went south, she'd also have to find a new roommate—she sure as hell wasn't going to continue living with him after a breakup.

And she didn't even know if he was interested. He hadn't shown any interest recently, and his plushie had just denied it, but then again, she'd made it clear last month that she didn't want to start up where they'd left off. Yet she couldn't help wondering…

Look, Rose, you're just charmed because he sent you a picture of his turtle, that's all. Ray is taking you on actual dates and buying you flowers, and the situation is much less complicated with him.

Yes, she just needed to spend more time with Ray, and her feelings for him would grow.

But when she was trying and failing to fall asleep that night—the futon wasn't the most comfortable—it was Cal's arms she thought of, not Ray's.

And if she was honest with herself, last Saturday, she'd had a better time baking cookies and watching TV with Cal than she'd had on her date with Ray.

~

Cal missed Rose, but he'd thought it was a little weird to say it, so he'd made Shelly say it to Fred instead. Surely that was normal.

And the main reason he missed Rose was because he couldn't watch *The Untamed* without her, wasn't it?

Although he'd been confused after the first few episodes, they'd now watched twenty-six, and he was very much into the adventures of Wei Wuxian. He supposed he could watch it by himself since she'd seen it multiple times before, but it would feel wrong.

So instead, he'd invited his sister and her family over on Saturday afternoon. Jodi had ended up bringing Kendall but not Riley; Riley had a baseball game, and her father had accompanied her. Though Kendall had spent much of the time on her phone, she'd liked Cal's new digs. Both his sister and his niece had been suspicious that his female roommate wasn't "just" a roommate, and the two of them agreeing on something was a novelty, so he'd managed a smile.

And now, Cal was spending Sunday morning trying to figure out what was going on with his finances and how much of his credit card debt he should pay this month. He was on his second cup of coffee, and he'd gotten nowhere. He'd printed out a bunch of things, thinking that might help, but the numbers still made no sense.

That brought back painful memories of sitting at the kitchen table with his father, Dad's frustration mounting as Cal failed, once again, at figuring out his math homework. His father was an engineering professor and numbers came easily to him, as well as to Cal's siblings—Jodi was an accountant.

Cal looked at the clock on his laptop and breathed out a sigh of relief. The financial mumbo-jumbo could wait until another day. It was eleven o'clock, which meant it was time to head out for dim sum with Peter So and his wife. Peter had invited him, and Cal felt a bit awkward about tagging along, but he had no idea what to order at dim sum without help.

When he got to the restaurant, he discovered it didn't have those cart thingies; rather, you had to order off the menu.

"We'll let Valerie pick," Peter said, putting a hand on her back. "She's the best at it." He looked at his wife fondly. "Why didn't you invite your roommate, Cal?"

Cal shrugged. Played it cool. "She's in Ottawa this weekend."

"Are you sure she's just a roommate?" Peter asked, waggling his eyebrows.

Great. Cal had gotten this from his family yesterday, and now his friend was giving him a hard time.

"Yeah," he said, "I'm sure."

"I think he's lying," Peter said to Valerie.

"Definitely," Valerie agreed, without taking her eyes off the menu.

"Men and women can be friends," Cal pointed out. "We're friends and roommates."

Sure, Rose caused some warm feelings in his chest at times, and sure, her ass looked great in her yoga pants, and sure, he missed her, now that he hadn't seen her in a couple of days.

Okay, maybe he did like her a little, as something other than a friend, but he wouldn't say it, even if Cal had a sneaking suspicion that the way he looked at Rose was a bit like the way Peter looked at Valerie.

$$[\ 15\ ]$$

Monday evening, Cal was sitting at the dining room table, staring at numbers on his laptop again. It didn't make any more damn sense than it had yesterday morning.

Rose walked by, wearing yoga pants and a tank top.

Dammit, it was getting harder and harder not to notice how hot she looked. Was it partly because as the weather warmed up, she wore less clothing?

Ugh. He needed to focus.

She went to the kitchen and came out a few minutes later with a cup of tea. "Want to watch a show?"

Oh, did he ever, but... "I have to finish this first."

"What are you working on?"

"Finances," he muttered. "I have some credit card debt and..."

"That's the worst. The interest rate is so high."

He returned to staring at the numbers but looked up a minute later, realizing she was still there.

"Do you need help?" she asked. "In the time we've lived together, I've never seen you look so..." She made a strange gesture. "Frustrated, I guess?"

He glanced at the screen then looked back at her. "I'm really bad with numbers."

Why was he telling her this? She was an engineer, like his dad. She wouldn't understand.

But he didn't shut up. "They never made sense to me, and basic stuff like paying bills and figuring out what to save is…hard."

That was part of the reason why he'd liked the idea of renting a place that included utilities. Fewer numbers to worry about, and he wouldn't have to concern himself with variations in hydro bills.

"Do you have dyscalculia?" she asked.

"Dis…what?"

"Dyscalculia. It's like…dyslexia for numbers. I don't know much about it, but…"

Huh. He'd never heard of that before.

"Anyway," she said, "whatever the reason, do you want me to help you? I don't know much about investing, but I can assist with interest rates and figuring out payments. Stuff like that."

"You don't need to." It was far beyond the job description of a roommate, and he wouldn't want her to lose whatever respect she had for him when she realized just how much he didn't understand.

She didn't say anything in response but stared pointedly at his hand, which was gripping his pen for dear life, rather like how his hands clenched when he thought of her going on a date. He wasn't really an anxious guy, but when it came to anything related to math, it was a different story. He couldn't help thinking of those long evenings at the kitchen table with his father, when Cal had never, ever lived up to expectations.

"We'll take half an hour and see what happens, okay?" Her voice was upbeat.

"Well…"

"If you don't want to share financial information with me, I get it, but I won't tell anything to anyone, and we'll do it all on your computer. I won't keep anything myself."

He did trust her, and unlike other people, she didn't seem at all judgmental—not yet anyway. Perhaps it was worth a try.

"Okay, but you don't know what you're getting into." He tried to smile.

"I'm sure it'll be fine." She shot him an easy grin as she sat down, and blood pumped to his groin. With her sitting here, maybe he was going to understand even less than usual.

He brought up his online banking, since he figured that would make things easier. He also showed her the small number of bills he had, plus his pay stubs.

She pulled up the spreadsheet program and split the screen so the browser was open on one half and the spreadsheet on the other. Her fingers flew across the keyboard, typing in the numbers he'd shown her, but somehow, they all made sense to her, unlike to him.

"I wasn't really stupid with my money," he said. "That's not why I have credit card debt." She hadn't asked, but he wanted her to know. "When I was younger, I sometimes offered to pay bills at the bar for my friends. It was on a credit card, so it seemed like it wasn't real money… Okay, I guess that is rather stupid. Then one time, I had to help Meena get out of a bad situation. But I learned my lesson, and when I inherited a small amount of money from my grandpa, I bought myself a car outright. No payment plan."

Her hands stopped moving and she looked at him like…well, he knew that look. It was the one people gave him when he did something particularly unintelligent. His dad had given him that look a *lot*.

Unlike his father, Rose quickly plastered it over with a smile. "It likely would have been better to use the money to pay off your credit card debt because those usually have the highest interest rates, so you'll end up paying more money over time. Whereas when you buy a new car, you can get a lower rate for a financing plan—although, to be fair, if you have a bad credit score, I'm not sure how much that would affect your options. It would have been worth doing some research, though, or waiting to buy a car if that was a possibility."

He didn't fully understand, so he hesitantly asked her to explain it again, which, to his surprise, she happily did without rolling her eyes.

Though now that he thought about it, he would have been surprised if she'd rolled her eyes, but he was instinctively expected her to act like other people had.

Without the looming possibility of her getting super annoyed or disappointed in him, he was actually sort of able to understand what was going on, even if her thigh was now pressing against his.

She did a calculation on the spreadsheet and said, "I think you should be able to pay it off within a year and a half." She paused. "Sorry, I don't think I explained everything as well as I could have. I'm not very good at teaching. My dad's great at it, but I don't have that talent."

He just stared at her. She thought this was a failing on *her* part?

"What?" she said.

"You're way better at this than most people."

"No, I—"

"You're patient and you don't think I'm an idiot."

"Oh," she said faintly, then tucked some hair behind her ear. "Uh, thank you."

"You're..." *You're amazing.*

But he didn't say that. It didn't seem appropriate, even if it was true.

"My dad always made me feel like an idiot," he heard himself saying. "He could never understand how things that were easy for him were hard for me."

"I can't pretend to know exactly what it's like. It *is* easy for me —I think that's why it's hard for me to explain things."

"But you're not weird and judgy about it like he is. My mom, too. She was always saying that she couldn't understand why I didn't try harder. Except I did try." And now that he thought about it, there were a few instances that made him wonder if his mother had the same issues as him and just did her best to hide it. Huh.

"We all have different strengths."

Cal had heard that one before, but it seemed more meaningful when Rose said it. He found himself leaning forward, as though he was about to kiss her.

He needed to get out of here before he did anything he shouldn't. "Thank you so much for your help. I gotta go, uh, make a call."

He took his laptop and sauntered upstairs. His brain urged him to move faster, but he didn't want to show how affected he was by her.

Since he didn't actually have a call to make, once he was in his bedroom, he googled "dyscalculia" and found long lists of things that he identified with more than a little.

Cal vaguely remembered something about warm milk helping you sleep, so when he was still awake at two thirty in the morning, he tiptoed downstairs and warmed up a small amount of milk in the microwave.

Insomnia was a rather unfamiliar experience, but his mind had been busy over the past few hours, thinking about how there was a name for his problem with numbers, rather than his dad just saying he was stupid, over and over.

Was it actually his parents who'd failed him, by not getting him the proper help? School hadn't been great, either, though he'd had one teacher—grade three?—who'd finally managed to teach him how to tell time, as well as some basic arithmetic.

But maybe there hadn't been much research about dyscalculia until recently? Huh. More stuff to look up.

After drinking his milk, he headed back upstairs and noticed a light on in what Rose called the "reading room." A small room with a reading nook that looked out onto the street.

He knocked on the door. "Rose?" He thought he heard some movement, but she didn't speak. "Are you okay?"

When he didn't hear anything more, he wondered if he should push open the door and check on her, or whether that would be an invasion of privacy.

Perhaps it was partly because he wasn't used to being up at two thirty in the morning and everything felt weird and quiet, but he started thinking the worst.

"Just tell me you're okay and I'll leave you alone," he said.

He heard nothing for a few long seconds, and then a quiet voice said, "Come in."

He entered carefully. Rose was sitting on the window seat, hugging a shark, a seal, and a sheep to her chest. She was staring out the window at the dark city, and she didn't seem like her usual self.

"I can't sleep. Again," she said.

He thought back to that night in August, when he'd found her crying on his couch, and his heart squeezed. She looked very different from the woman who'd helped with his finances several hours earlier. Unlike last summer, she wasn't crying, but she looked vacant.

He crouched down on the floor next to her and wrapped his arms around her. She buried her head in his shoulder, and one of the stuffed animals fell out of her lap and onto the floor, but she didn't move to pick it up. She just stayed there, like she was comfortable in his arms.

"I suffer from depression," she said, "and I have anxiety, too.

Sometimes in the middle of the night, my mind just keeps spinning, and I feel hollow inside. The longer I'm awake, the more tired I get, but the wider awake I feel. Usually, I don't get to this point, not as often as I used to, but..."

"And this time, it's not because you're trying to share a bed with me, or because you don't have anything to hold." But perhaps he shouldn't have referenced that night.

She didn't seem bothered by his words, though. "Even my optimal sleeping conditions aren't always enough."

He took a moment to process everything she'd just told him. "What can I do?"

"Nothing," she said miserably. "It's not like anyone can solve all my problems. I've tried so many things...it's just the way it is." Her voice was a little flat.

"But right now, what would make you the tiniest bit less spinny or empty?"

She chuckled weakly, not like the way she sometimes laughed, but it was precious nonetheless.

"You only have a shark, a seal, and a sheep here," he said, "but I could get you others. Your alpaca and sloth, and I think you also have an ice cream cone plushie. That might distract the shark from eating the seal."

"He's a nice shark. He doesn't eat anyone."

"Even nice sharks need food. You know, there's probably a store open at this time that sells plushies." He didn't know what he was saying; he just felt the need to fill the silence, hoping something would amuse her.

And to distract him from how wonderful she felt in his arms. It seemed wrong to notice that when she clearly wasn't in a good place. He desperately wished he could take all of it away from her, but if she didn't have a solution, he doubted he could come up with one, especially since he knew little of what she was going through.

"If there was a shop down the street," he said, "I'd buy you a plush slice of pepperoni pizza."

"Mmm." She relaxed against him.

They stayed there in the semi-darkness for a while—he had no concept of time right now—and then Rose said, "I should go back to bed."

They headed to their bedrooms. His mind was quieter now, and he hoped hers was, too.

When his head hit the pillow, he fell right to sleep.

Rose woke up at seven the next morning, after an insufficient three and a half hours of sleep. She went downstairs and found coffee in the coffeemaker, as usual. But Cal had made her extra coffee, and there was also a note on the table, next to Shelly: *Shelly wishes you a good day at work.*

Even though Rose was tired and felt a heavy weight on her chest, the note still made her smile. The extra coffee helped, too.

Work was okay, considering she hadn't slept enough. Perhaps it was all the caffeine she'd consumed, but when she got home at six, she was the most awake she'd been all day, and Cal was outside, weeding their small flower garden.

This was most unfair.

Her libido had been completely absent in the middle of the night when he'd had his arms around her, but it roared back now. He was wearing shorts and a white tank top, which gave her an extremely good view of his biceps, and the way the sunlight hit his brown hair made it look like it was threaded with gold.

And he was so *sweet.* Honestly, that was the sexiest part.

"Hey, Rose," he said, standing up when he saw her. "How was your day?"

"It was alright," she said. "Considering."

He nodded. "Cool. You want me to make something for dinner?"

His offer to take care of dinner was even more of a turn-on. Seriously, what was wrong with her?

At her silence, he stepped closer to her—which didn't help matters at all, of course. His biceps were at eye level; she tilted her head up, but that easy smile on his face was just as sexy.

He hadn't slept well last night, either, and then he'd gone to his manual labor job. How could he look so damn good after all that? She knew she looked far from her best, and the concealer she'd reapplied at lunch was probably doing a bad job of hiding the circles under her eyes.

She should decline his offer to figure out dinner, but her tired body and mind wouldn't let her. "That would be great, thank you. I'm just going to, uh, visit Amy first. Be back in an hour."

That wouldn't be enough to douse her desire for him, but hopefully it would help a little.

Amy answered her door, the baby balanced on her hip. "Is something wrong?"

Was Amy asking that because of how Rose looked? Or because she never showed up unannounced like this?

"No," Rose said, "I'm fine. Yes, I'm fine. I just thought I could use some Hudson time. What do you think?" She addressed this last part to the baby, who giggled.

"You mind if I take a shower while you hold him?" Amy asked. "Victor's still at work."

Soon, Rose and Hudson were sitting together in the armchair in the front room. Rose knew she wouldn't cope well with a baby of her own, but she did like babies.

"Is that a dinosaur onesie, Hudson? How cute. What's your favorite dinosaur? T-Rex? Triceratops? Pachycephalosaurus?"

He giggled in that delightful way babies had.

"Do you think it's a funny word? Pachycephalosaurus?"

He giggled again and tried to grab her glasses, so she put those aside. There was a small lion toy on the coffee table, and she handed it to him. He promptly stuck it in his mouth.

"How do you think Cal feels about me?" she asked.

Hudson looked at her curiously, then decided her question didn't merit an answer. He pulled the toy out of his mouth and shook it around before biting on it again.

"But I'm not sure it matters," she went on. "It's too risky, isn't it? He broke my heart once before, and we barely knew each other then. If it happens again, especially now that we're living together…"

"Ba!" Hudson said triumphantly, handing her his toy.

"Why, thank you. You're such a sweetheart."

Hudson smiled, well aware of just how sweet he was, then apparently decided he was too sweet and started fussing.

He did a good job of distracting Rose, but when she returned home and saw Cal in the kitchen, washing lettuce, all her desire for him returned.

How was *washing lettuce* sexy?

God, she was screwed.

THAT SATURDAY at the cider bar, Rose ordered a glass of the passionfruit peach cider, since she was craving something sweet. Her roommate immediately popped into her head again—had he ever really left?—and she tried, once again, to push him out.

And once again, she wasn't successful.

"What's wrong, Rose?" Sierra asked, leaning forward.

Rose looked around at her friends: Sierra, Nicole, and Charlotte. Amy wasn't here tonight—she was catching up on sleep instead. Rose had known these three women for over a decade. She'd hung out with them somewhat regularly at university, and when she'd decided to move to Toronto, they'd gotten closer. These women had helped her through a lot. She shouldn't be nervous about telling them about Cal, but she was.

Charlotte opened her mouth before Rose could say anything. "Is it Cal? What did that fucker do?"

Rose chuckled. "It's not what you think. He's a good roommate."

"Oh?" Nicole said.

"Yeah. That's the problem. The more he cooks for me, the more weeds he pulls out, the more episodes of *The Untamed* we watch together…the more I want to jump his bones." She covered her face after saying the last words; she wasn't used to talking about her sexual desires.

And the way he allowed himself to be vulnerable with her, and let her know just how difficult figuring out his finances was —that touched her, too.

But he wasn't acting like this because she was anyone special to him, right? He was just a kind person, and they lived together. Maybe she shouldn't read much into things.

Except…

"What about Ray?" Sierra asked.

Oh, God. Ray.

Rose liked him, too, and things were going well so far. They'd gone out for dinner again two nights ago, and today, he'd sent her flowers. Not red roses, but a mixed bouquet, and it had made her a little giddy, though not as much as last time.

"I guess I should see what happens with Ray first," Rose said.

"You guess," Nicole repeated.

"Yeah."

"What's the worst that could happen if you ask Cal how he feels about you?"

"Well." Rose had given this a lot of thought. "There are so many terrible options. He could say he doesn't have any feelings for me, and then things could get awkward between us, especially if he starts bringing someone else home. What if it gets so awkward that one of us has to move? The thought is over-whelming right now and—"

"Nicole," Charlotte said. "I can't believe you asked Rose about worst-case scenarios. She thinks about that all the time, and she always gets to death or the end of the world pretty quickly. Besides, it wasn't all that long ago that you were scared of being with David, scared of losing yourself in a relationship."

"I'm not scared of that," Rose said.

"But I'm sure you make up for it with your other fears."

"I do." She looked down at her cider.

In general, she wasn't scared of relationships. She wanted one. But with Cal, it was extra complicated, especially since she already knew what it was like for him to break her heart. She wasn't afraid of heartbreak, except when it came to him.

Weird.

Besides, did she really like Cal more than Ray? Or was it just that she knew him better?

"I think you should wear a really sexy outfit around Cal and see what he does," Nicole said. "We'll go shopping together. I'll find you something."

"Uh…" Rose said.

"I've seen pictures of this guy. He's hot. I understand the appeal, although he never called you last year."

"I believe his story about his phone getting run over by a truck. I know it sounds far-fetched, but I do. And when I couldn't sleep the other night, he left extra coffee for me in the morning and a note from Shelly."

"Who's Shelly?" Charlotte asked.

"His stuffed turtle. She has an Instagram account, and she and Fred have adventures together. The other day, Cal bought a slice of roll cake from Harbord Coffee Bar, and we took pictures of our plushies with the cake before we ate it. Shelly's bio says she likes cake, you see."

Her friends all looked at each other.

"What?" Rose asked. "I know it's childish, but I like—"

"There is no way this guy isn't in love with you," Sierra said decisively.

Rose experienced a moment of incandescent hope, which quickly disappeared. "Nah, it's just the kind of guy he is. I've seen him with other people."

"I know there are risks," Nicole said, "but I think you should say something to him. If he turns you down, you can do your best to pretend the conversation never happened."

Rose didn't see herself having great success with that.

"At least you'll know," Nicole continued. "You won't always wonder."

"But what if I like Ray more?"

Nicole raised an *are-you-kidding-me?* eyebrow.

"Ray is the more...sensible choice," Rose said hesitantly. "There isn't the complication of us living together."

She started laughing. Here she was, trying to decide between two guys. Was this her life?

Of course, it wasn't as if she could be sure they both liked her. In fact, she was pretty doubtful of Cal's feelings, but Ray was taking her out on dates and sending her flowers. She knew he was interested.

She wouldn't push her luck and ask Cal what he thought of her. She should be happy with what she had, which was pretty damn good. Sure, there had been that one moment when she'd found Ray's smile a little odd, but she pushed that aside once more. It was just her brain misfiring again.

"Colton sounded like a good choice, too," Sierra said. "On paper, he was the dream guy, but...ugh."

"Well, I'll spend time getting to know Ray better," Rose said. "I won't do anything rash."

Nicole still looked skeptical, but whatever. Rose and Nicole were very different people.

"Does your dad inquire about your dating life?" Sierra asked. "Does he make comments about when you're *finally* going to get married? I know your father would be much nicer about it than my parents, but still."

Rose shook her head. "I told him not to ask aboout it, so he doesn't."

Nicole choked on her drink. "You told him not to ask, and *he actually listens*? Really? He doesn't bug you about it even more?"

"Nope."

"Wow," Sierra said. "Can't imagine what that's like. I knew

your relationship with your dad was much different than my relationship with my mom, but…"

Rose shrugged. "When there's news, I'll tell him. In Ottawa, I got a text and Dad asked me if it was a guy, but that was it. He's never intrusive about that sort of thing."

"And as a result, you're not going to wait a whole year to tell him when you get a boyfriend. See, I wish my mom would realize that's the secret for getting me to actually tell her things, as opposed to calling me multiple times a day."

Rose's mom had definitely been different from her father in this respect, but not quite like any of her friends' parents.

Rose swallowed some more cider and acknowledged the twinge in her chest. It would never go away completely, and she'd learned to live with it and accept it. Mostly. She imagined setting it aside in a box for now, then looked toward the spot where she'd tripped and encountered Ray for the first time.

Yes, that had certainly been a romantic way to meet. She looked forward to the next date…and she also looked forward to going home and seeing Cal.

But until then, she'd enjoy this time with her friends and try not to focus on her confusion, though she was certain she wouldn't fully succeed.

Sierra put a hand on Rose's back. "You okay?

"Yeah," Rose said. "I'm okay. I think."

She had no plans to say anything to Cal, but at least she felt a little less freaked out about the whole thing now, although maybe that was just because she wasn't in his presence.

"Wow, look at you," Cal said, slapping Marv on the back. "Only five minutes late."

"Hey, five minutes late counts as on time in my books," Marv said.

"Same, same."

Several months ago, Marv had discovered that he had ADHD, and he now knew the term for his issues with time: time blindness. He was better at managing it than he used to be but still struggled. Meeting at Cal's place made things simple because Cal could easily occupy himself if Marv was late, though it hadn't been an issue today.

Cal cracked open a beer for each of them, and they sat down on the couch, the game on in the background.

"Is Rose around tonight?" Marv asked.

"Nah. She has plans with her friends."

"How's it going with her? The living arrangement working out okay?"

"Yeah, it's good," Cal said. "She's amazing."

"Amazing, you say. Sounds like someone has a crush."

Cal shrugged. Maybe he did. So what.

"You sleeping together?" Marv asked.

"No, just baking cookies and watching TV, that sort of thing." Cal spoke casually, as though this was all normal.

But with Rose, everything seemed a little better than ordinary.

"You know how I've always been bad at math?" he said suddenly. "She thinks I have something called dyscalculia, and I think she's right. She's so smart—she knows all sorts of things. Like, she figured out I was baking my cookies in Fahrenheit when the recipe was in Celsius."

Marv bent over and laughed, and Cal smacked him with a pillow.

"She doesn't laugh at me as much as your ass does," Cal said.

"Sorry, sorry. Just imagining you surrounded by undercooked cookies, holding a spatula and trying to figure out what's going on. But that dis-whatever thing is interesting. Never heard of that."

"Neither had I."

"So, whatcha going to do about Rose?" Marv asked. "You've been with her before, so you know what the sex is like."

"I don't know, man. She was acting weird the other day when I was weeding the garden, like she didn't want to get too close to me, and then she went on a date with someone else last night. Guess we'll just see what happens."

But Cal was less easygoing about things than usual.

He knew exactly what he wanted; he just didn't know what *she* wanted—though the fact that she was going on dates with Ray and receiving flowers from him seemed like a sign.

Not one in Cal's favor.

Whatever. He'd try not to worry about it too much.

$$[\ 17\ ]$$

TUESDAY EVENING AFTER DINNER, Cal was watching *The Untamed* with Rose. They only had a few episodes left. The show was going in places he hadn't expected, but he supposed it was quite different from anything he'd watched before.

All of a sudden, everything went black. The TV shut off. The lights went out.

"Shit," Rose said from somewhere to his right.

They were both quiet for a few moments, and then he heard her get up. His heart pounded, but her footsteps on the creaky old floor moved farther away.

Why had he thought she was going to sit on his lap? What a silly idea.

He heard her open the front door before she returned to the living room.

"Looks like all the lights on the street are out," she said. "It's not just us."

Well, not a problem for them to worry about, then.

"Shit," she said again. "I have lots of food in the fridge. I don't want it to go to waste. And the freezer…"

"The frozen stuff will keep for a while."

"Forty-eight hours. That's how long you have for the freezer. For the fridge, I think it's only four or five hours."

"We've got time. The power will probably be back on within an hour. We can check the hydro company's website in a few minutes to see if they have an update."

"The year of the ice storm," she said. "Do you remember that? I think it was 2013. I'd just moved to Toronto, and my power was out for four days before Christmas. I lost all my food. Well, maybe some things would have been okay since it was cold outside, but I didn't want to risk it."

"But this outage isn't caused by a storm. It shouldn't be out for days."

"I know. I just…"

"You want to go for a walk?" he asked. "It would give us something to do rather than use up our phone batteries."

"Good idea."

The lights were out when they got to Bloor, but when they walked a few blocks west, everything was lit up again. It was rare for Cal to be out with Rose—it hadn't happened since the night he'd brought her to the pub—and it was kind of thrilling. It shouldn't feel like a big deal, but it was.

"Ooh." She stopped in front of a bubble tea shop. "Do you want brown sugar boba?"

"Say what?"

"You've never had it before?"

"I've had bubble tea, but not that kind." He patted his pockets. "I don't have my wallet."

"That's okay. I'll buy."

He made a note on his phone to pay her back while she went to buy their drinks. They looked pretty cool, with the dark tapioca balls at the bottom, followed by streaks of brown in pale liquid. He was about to pierce the top with his straw when she put her hand on his wrist.

His brain might not be good at, say, mental math, but it was excellent at remembering all the little ways they'd touched in the past few weeks. The most recent time had been when he'd found her awake in the middle of the night and put his arm around her —a much longer touch than this, but he was still very aware of this one.

"Sorry, could you repeat that?" he said, realizing words had come out of her mouth.

"I always shake it up before drinking, but you should take your pretty pictures of it now."

He rarely took pictures, but he took one of his drink. When he noticed her staring at him, she quickly looked away.

"Let's, uh, walk while we have our boba," she said.

"The hydro company's website says the power will be back in an hour or two."

He was prepared for her to freak out that it wouldn't be on soon, but she didn't, perhaps reassured that their food wouldn't be at risk.

He gave his cup a vigorous shake and started drinking as they ambled down a side street. "Wow, this is good."

"I know, right? It's my favorite."

He made a mental note of that.

Well, Ray, she's having bubble tea with me tonight, not you.

The other day, Rose had been smiling while talking to someone on the phone, and Cal had briefly wondered if it was Ray. When he'd realized it was her dad, he'd been more relieved than he should have been. He just couldn't help it with her, and they hadn't spent much time together lately, except when they were watching *The Untamed.*

Rose looked up at the sky. "I guess I'm in the mood for thinking about the past today. Remember the blackout in 2003? I could see so many stars. It was like going camping."

"You lost power in Ottawa, too?"

"Yeah. I was at the mall with my mom, and it took us forever to drive back because all the traffic lights were out." This was the first time he'd heard her mention her mother. "At night, my dad pointed out all the constellations to us."

"Well, I was younger than you, maybe ten or eleven. I don't remember it well, to be honest."

"Ugh, I feel weird."

"Why?" he asked.

"You're so much younger than me!"

"I thought it was six years?" He recalled her mentioning the other day that she was thirty-five. "It's not that much."

"Oh, God. you were in middle school when I was in university!"

"But I'm not in middle school anymore," he said, his voice low.

She stopped on the sidewalk. They were on a residential street that didn't have any power, so he couldn't see her face as well as he wanted. But he'd be able to touch...

He clenched his hand—the one that wasn't holding the bubble tea—into a fist so he didn't reach toward her.

"Who cares if roommates are six years apart?" he said lightly. "It's no big deal."

"You know what I'm talking about."

"Nah, I really have no idea."

She gave him a shove. "Dammit, you're too big and solid. I can't..."

"I'm too big, Rose?"

"Shut up. You're too big *for me to push*."

"I see, I see."

"Shut up," she said again.

He wished the lights would come back on. He wished it were daylight so he could see the expression on her face—and whether her cheeks were a lovely shade of pink. But since he couldn't see her as well as he'd like, he stepped closer instead. He didn't touch her, just stood near her, and he was rewarded with her sharp intake of breath.

"So you're talking about the fact that we had sex, Rose? You feel weird for sleeping with a younger guy?"

"How old did you think I was when we met?"

"Same age as me, maybe a year or two older? I didn't think about it much." He shrugged and leaned toward her. "You enjoyed yourself, didn't you?"

He couldn't help pushing her a little, just to see what she'd do. He suddenly had a feeling that she'd been spending less time with him lately *because* she was attracted to him.

Thank God for blackouts.

"Do you think about that night much?" he asked.

If she said no, he wouldn't push any further, but…

"Yes," she whispered.

He hissed out a breath. "What parts do you think about? Tell me." He was very aware of the rise and fall of her chest underneath that tank top. "Do you think about how angry you were when I took your seat? Or do you think more about what happened when—"

She leaned forward and kissed him.

Maybe she was trying to shut him up more than anything, but he didn't care. She wrapped her arms around him, pressing her body and her lips to his. He slipped his hands into her hair and kissed her back, his empty bubble tea cup falling to the sidewalk. She tasted of brown sugar boba and *Rose*.

And then her lips left his.

"That was okay?" she asked.

"Of course."

"You still want to kiss me, even now that you know what I'm really like?"

He frowned. "Why wouldn't I?"

At that, she kissed him harder, both of her hands coming up to cup his face, and it felt like she was putting everything she had into the kiss. He slipped one hand around her waist, just under the hem of her shirt so he could feel her bare skin—he was desperate to touch her. To be closer to her. To feel her hands on his hardening length.

"Rose," he murmured as her lips trailed down his neck before returning to his mouth.

But as soon as his tongue touched hers, she leapt back from him and ran in the direction of their home.

[18]

OMG I kissed Cal. OMG I kissed Cal. OMG I kissed Cal.

Rose was glad to discover that the porchlight was on—it meant they had power. She hurried inside, toed off her sandals, ran upstairs to her bedroom, and shut the door.

She'd kissed him so he'd stop talking. So he wouldn't say anything about how he'd finger-fucked her behind the bar. Except kissing him had been the wrong way to solve that problem, especially since it had been just as good as she'd remembered, possibly even better, and it had made her feel things she hadn't felt in a long time. What had she been thinking?

She hadn't been thinking, that was the problem.

And now she'd kissed her roommate, and she had to keep living with him.

She slid down to the floor in front of her bedroom door and leaned back against it. It was the stupid blackout's fault. If it hadn't been for the power going out, they would have finished their episode of *The Untamed*. Then she would have gone upstairs and read a little. She was reading a steampunk novel now and...

Oh, God.

That made her think of Cal, too. Of the night they'd met, once again.

But she hadn't been able to leave everything in the past. She'd kissed him, and he'd seemed very happy to kiss her back, but when he'd used his tongue, she'd remembered that tongue being in other places.

Oh, God, what had she done?

She'd told herself that even though she was attracted to Cal, she wasn't going to do anything about it. It was too risky, and besides, she was already dating Ray.

How had she forgotten about Ray?

She picked up her phone and did something she never, ever did: she called a friend. Called, not texted.

"Rose?" Nicole said. "Is everything okay?"

"The power went out and Cal and I went for a walk and got bubble tea and I kissed him and then I ran home." As she said it, she heard the front door open. He was here. "And now the power is on, and oh my God, I cheated on Ray!"

"You didn't cheat. You've been on two dates, and I can't imagine you've talked about being exclusive."

"No…"

"You did nothing wrong."

"Did you hear me? I kissed Cal. He's my roommate, and it was already weird, and now it's going to be even weirder."

"Was it a good kiss?" Nicole asked.

"It doesn't matter."

"So it was good."

"Stop smirking!" Rose cried.

"Why do you think I'm smirking? You can't see me. This isn't a video call."

"I can just tell."

"Rose," Nicole said soothingly. "Why did you kiss him?"

"Because he was pissing me off!"

Nicole's laughter traveled over the phone.

You still want to kiss me, even now that you know what I'm really like?

Why wouldn't I?

Those words came back to Rose now. The circumstances of tonight's kiss had been completely different from their first kiss, all those months ago. Then, they'd been strangers at a bar. That was before she'd cried on his couch in the middle of the night. Before he'd seen her enormous collection of plushies. Before...so many things.

He didn't know everything about her, no, but he knew her pretty well, and that hadn't turned him off.

There was a soft knock on her door. She startled.

"Rose, are you okay?" Cal asked.

"Yes!" she called out, louder than necessary considering they were separated only by her door.

"I'll be in my room if you need me."

She stayed silent as he padded away.

"Were you just talking to him?" Nicole asked.

"He was checking up on me," Rose replied. "He's gone now. I can't believe I've kissed two guys in the past few weeks. Two!"

"Who was better?"

"Nicole!"

"What, it's a fair question. Not that 'who is the better kisser?' is the only consideration, but still."

"Cal," Rose said, before she could think better of it. God, what was with her today?

But she couldn't risk him breaking her heart again. That would be too much for her, and she was in a fragile place mentally, even if things were better than they'd been in the winter. Besides, she didn't even know what Cal wanted.

"But you still want to see what happens with Ray?" Nicole asked. "Are you sure?"

"Yes." Rose felt a moment of disappointment after saying that word, but she pushed it aside.

"Whatever happens, we'll be there for you. You know that, don't you?"

"Yes." Rose smiled weakly. "I know."

But the worst she could feel was a very scary place, and she had to do her best to avoid it.

~

Cal stared at the TV. "Wow. That was amazing."

"It was, wasn't it?" Rose said.

He'd been a little skeptical he'd enjoy a fifty-episode show that had confused him so thoroughly at the beginning, but he'd agreed to watch it because…well.

Because he had a thing for Rose, and he wanted to learn more about what she enjoyed.

But as it turned out, he'd liked it quite a bit.

He hated that it was over, and he feared they'd spend less time together now. Things had become more awkward since the power outage two days ago. She seemed to be making even more of an effort to avoid him, and he was giving her whatever space she needed, even if it wasn't what he wanted.

She was clearly rattled by the kiss, and he wanted to comfort her, like he had the night she couldn't sleep, but he knew he was the wrong person for that. He didn't know what he ought to do but figured it was best to take his cues from her.

It was just difficult when all he wanted was to hold her. And to slide the strap of her tank top down her shoulder…

"Do you want to watch another Asian drama together?" she asked.

"Yes," he said immediately.

"I'll send you a few titles, and you can look them up and decide which you'd prefer."

"Sounds good."

Whatever one has more episodes. That way I can spend the most time with you.

"Maybe we can start it tomorrow," he said. "What would you like for dinner? We can—"

"No, I have a date."

"With Ray?"

"Yeah."

Cal couldn't help thinking about their kiss two nights ago, and he was positive she was thinking about it, too.

How can you go on a date with him after that?

He wouldn't ask her that, however. She'd get annoyed with him.

That night, when Cal climbed into bed, his mind drifted to what would happen if she were in his bed. If she let him kiss her in other places: her throat, her shoulder, her breasts. If she arched against him and pushed his head between her legs...

That's right, Rose. Let me give you what you want. Let me take care of you.

He had to jerk himself off before he could sleep.

"Hey, man, what's up with you today?" Peter asked Cal.

"Nothing's up," Cal growled, stabbing the soil with his shovel.

Okay, he could see Peter's point. He wasn't acting like his usual self.

"She's going on a date tonight," Cal said.

"Not with you, I presume?"

Cal didn't bother responding.

"This is your roommate?" Peter asked. "The one who's definitely nothing more than a roommate? That one?"

Cal shot him a murderous look.

God, he really wasn't himself at work today, and he hated it. And he wasn't looking forward to going home, either. There was no way in hell he could stand to be around when Rose got ready for her date, especially if Ray was going to pick her up.

Nope, Cal would go out, maybe get drunk. That seemed like the best plan. Maybe Peter would be willing to join him.

But what if Ray spent the night?

[19]

PENGUIN PIP: *Looking good, Fred! I love the bow. It's so sparkly.*

Merry Lamb: *I haven't seen you hanging out with Shelly lately.*

Fred the Alpaca: *Shelly has spent the last week walking up the stairs. You know how slow turtles can be.*

Penguin Pip: *Did your humans have a fight?*

Fred the Alpaca: *No.*

Rose tossed her third necklace aside. Nothing she put on was quite right. She wasn't usually so indecisive about what to wear, but then again, she didn't usually have a roiling mass in her gut.

Though she was no stranger to anxiety, this seemed different from normal. She supposed it was because she had this idea—where she'd gotten it, she wasn't sure—that the third date was often when people slept together.

Except she wasn't ready to sleep with Ray.

She put a few condoms in her purse, just in case she changed her mind, and she was heading down the stairs when the doorbell rang.

She opened it to reveal Ray. He'd wanted to pick her up tonight, and she'd figured she was comfortable with that now. He was wearing a suit, no tie, shirt open at the collar.

"You look nice," he said.

"So do you."

See? It was easy to say stuff like that to him. It wasn't a lie, even if he didn't make her heart pound quite the way Cal did.

Ray took her to a Portuguese restaurant a little west of where she lived. A place with white linen tablecloths and servers in perfectly pressed shirts. She'd heard of this restaurant and had wanted to go here for a while, but she hadn't because it was rather expensive and it also seemed like the sort of place you went to on a date, not with friends.

But tonight, she *was* on a date.

There was lots of seafood on the menu. They decided to split the grilled squid as an appetizer, and when it arrived, it looked amazing. Rose was about to spear a piece with her fork when Ray said, "Would you mind if I took a picture?"

"No, go right ahead." She totally understood the impulse to take pictures of food, especially when it looked as pretty on the plate as this did.

He took a photo, then slipped his phone back into his pocket. "I'll put it on Instagram later," he said, and she appreciated that he wasn't going to spend any more time on his phone now.

She bit into a piece of squid and groaned. Yeah, that was incredible. She didn't miss how Ray focused on her lips as she enjoyed her food.

"Do you have an Instagram account?" he asked. "I'll follow you."

"Yes! Well, sort of. My alpaca has an account."

"Your alpaca? I think I misheard."

"No, I have a stuffed alpaca named Fred, and I take pictures of him wearing pretty ribbons, drinking boba..." She trailed off when she saw the expression on Ray's face.

"Is this a favorite childhood toy?" he asked.

"No, I got Fred a couple of years ago from my friend's store. I take pictures of him with my other plushies, too, but he's the star of the account."

Ray seemed perplexed, and she understood. She was an adult; she wasn't supposed to love stuffed animals so much. He'd probably be appalled that she slept with one and found it comforting.

But he'd eventually accept her love of plushies, right? Even if he didn't understand it?

Suddenly, she started to worry about all the things she'd have to tell him sooner rather than later. How would he react when he found out she was depressed? Would he assume she just wasn't trying hard enough to get better? What would he say when she told him about her mother? When she told him that she could never carry a pregnancy because the toll it would take on her would be too great?

That was when it hit her: she didn't want Ray to get to know her better. The idea of opening up to him was scary—and it wasn't the sort of fear that she knew she should push past. Her gut was telling her *no*, and this time, she would listen. He wasn't the right guy for her.

On the other hand, she felt comfortable with Cal; she didn't fear telling him things, and he often understood her without being told. That was rare, and she shouldn't dismiss her feelings just because he was her roommate. Because he'd once—in a bout of rotten luck—gotten his phone run over by a truck. They were very different people, but he still *got* her. Rather than laughing at Fred's Instagram account, he'd bought a stuffed turtle, and when she'd had a bad night, he'd left her a note from his turtle.

She couldn't deny how she felt about him any longer.

As Rose became aware of her surroundings again, she realized that Ray was eating more than his share of squid.

That wasn't acceptable.

She grabbed the biggest piece and stuffed it in her mouth, but she struggled to swallow. She didn't want to be here with Ray, though she did want to eat the seabass she'd ordered. This place was supposed to have good desserts, too.

Rose had just decided to wait out dinner when his hand brushed her knee under the table, and she stiffened.

"What's the matter, Rose?"

She heard him say it with a sneer, but maybe that was just her imagination. She pushed his hand away, and he didn't try to touch her again.

The server came to clear their dishes, and Rose waited until he was gone before saying, "Look, I'm really sorry, but I don't think this is going to work out." She gestured between her and Ray.

He wiped his mouth with his napkin. "You were just using me to enjoy some nice meals."

She tensed. "What? No. I can pay my half."

"Let me guess. There's someone else, isn't there?"

"Actually—"

"That white guy you live with, right?" He snorted. "Figures. I thought you were different, but you're not. You're just like all the Asian girls who won't date Asian guys."

This wasn't the reaction she'd expected. She gripped the seat of her chair with both hands. "Um...I dated you?"

"You were using me."

"No, I really thought it might work out! I went on the dates because I liked you."

"But if a white guy shows any interest, you're always going to pick him." Ray shook his head. "You have it so easy."

Welp. She was on a date with an MRAsian.

"You think our lives are better than yours," she said, "because some white men fetishize Asian women?"

"Poor you," he said sarcastically. Patronizingly. "You're a traitor."

"Yeah, poor me indeed. I'm on a date with *you*," Rose shot

back—most unlike her—just as the server arrived with their meals.

Now she had a decision to make: what the hell should she do with her food? It was exquisitely plated and smelled delicious. She wanted to take a picture then eat it, but she sure didn't want to do that in the company of Ray.

There were a lot more words on the tip of her tongue. It was instinctive to defend herself and point out that her longest relationship—fifteen years ago now, but still—had been with an Asian guy. And that, if anything, she'd imagined she'd marry an Asian guy; it had seemed likely that such a man would better understand certain aspects of her and her family. She also had things to say about Ray's lack of respect for Asian women.

What was the point, though? He wasn't going to change his mind because of anything she said. Why put herself through all that?

"Excuse me," she said to the server, just as he turned to walk away. She shot him a smile that she would no longer spare for Ray. "Could you box this up for me? Then I'll pay for it—just my main course. Thank you."

"Certainly," he said, though Rose thought he looked unimpressed that she was taking her food to go. This was not the kind of restaurant from which people took doggy bags, but she was going to pay for her food and eat it, dammit.

"You're causing a scene," Ray hissed.

"Me?" she whisper-shouted. "*Me?*"

"Just because I didn't approve of you having an Instagram account for your stuffed alpaca."

There really was no point in talking to this guy.

She quickly texted Charlotte, asking if Charlotte and Mike—who lived nearby and had recently bought a car—could pick her up ASAP. Even trying to use Uber seemed too complicated right now, and Rose could use a familiar face.

The server returned and she paid the bill, her fingers shaking on her credit card. Then she grabbed her food and hurried outside without looking to see if anyone in the restaurant was staring at her.

She found a nearby coffee shop and bought a tea while she waited for Charlotte. Her hands were still shaking, and when her friend came through the door, Rose started sobbing, the adrenaline she'd felt earlier completely disappearing.

"What did he do?" Charlotte demanded as she helped Rose into the back seat of the car.

Rose fumbled with her seatbelt before telling Charlotte what had happened at dinner.

"That fucker," Charlotte muttered. "He knows where you live, right?"

Yeah, even before he'd picked Rose up tonight, he'd known. She'd given him her address because he'd said he wanted to send her something, and then she'd received the roses.

"I don't think he'll do anything," she said. Though, in retrospect, telling Ray where she lived—before they'd gone on a single date—hadn't been the brightest idea. But, maybe because she hadn't dated in so long, that hadn't occurred to her earlier. "Besides, Cal is there."

Cal. Yes. She'd been thinking about him when she'd told Ray that it wasn't going to work out, but then her brain had been consumed with Ray's comments and the realization that he was a piece of shit.

Sure, Ray had a point—Asian men sometimes had it tough in the dating world. He'd said that before. But it didn't mean Rose owed him anything.

And his biggest problem for dating? He was an entitled asshole.

Damn, she should have listened to her instincts when she'd thought there was something a bit off with Ray. It was just difficult to trust herself at times.

"I'm so sorry," she said to Charlotte and Mike. "I'm sure you had plans for the night."

"Shut it," Charlotte said. "Texting me was the right thing to do. Now…ooh, there's a parking spot."

Mike parked a few houses down from where Rose lived. She clutched the doggy bag to her chest as she walked up the stairs to the house. Mike and Charlotte followed.

"You don't need to…" Rose began, but then she realized that all the lights were out. Not surprising. Cal hadn't been home when she'd left, and she'd only been gone just over an hour. She'd feel better having company until he returned.

Rose didn't text him, much as she wished to see him. She didn't want him to rush home, and she still had her dinner to eat. She opened up the box, sat on the couch, and stared at the food. It didn't look nearly as pretty as it had at the restaurant.

"You want me to get you a fork?" Charlotte asked.

Right. Utensils would be good.

Rose nodded. "You can also open the white wine in the fridge."

Charlotte returned with the wine bottle, two wineglasses, and a fork. While she poured the wine, Rose hugged her sloth plushie to her chest before trying a bite of fish. It didn't taste like it was worth what she'd paid for it, but that wasn't the restaurant's fault. She considered not finishing her meal, then decided she ought to have some sustenance.

Yes, she needed to focus on the basics for now. Staying safe. Food and water. A small glass of wine, no more. Deep breath in, deep breath out.

"So," Charlotte said, "you like Cal after all?"

"I do," Rose said.

But when she confessed her feelings, what would he say?

$$[\ 20\ ]$$

Something wasn't right.

When Cal stepped into the house, he heard unfamiliar voices. Had Rose brought Ray back to the house without telling him? They'd promised to give each other a head's up about guests, but maybe she thought it wasn't necessary because she'd told him she had a date.

But then he realized there were *two* unfamiliar voices.

He took off his shoes and stepped into the living room. A man and woman he'd never met before were there, and Rose was sitting on the couch with a glass of wine. Her date must have gone poorly, but Cal couldn't be happy about that when she looked so miserable.

"Rose?" he said hesitantly.

She jerked her head up, and a whole bunch of emotions passed over her face. He was usually good at reading her, but not now; he wasn't sure what was going on. Maybe it was because he'd had more than a couple of drinks with Peter. He hadn't gotten drunk after all—it took quite a bit to get him drunk—but his brain was fuzzier than usual.

"We'll go, if that's okay?" the woman said.

When Rose nodded, the two strangers left, and Cal sat down on the couch beside her.

"What happened?" he asked softly.

Rose hesitated, and his heart pounded in the silence.

"I realized I didn't like Ray," she said at last, and he refrained from pumping his fist. "He asked if I had an Instagram account, and when I told him about Fred, he thought I was a weirdo."

"You're not weird. Well, maybe you are, but in a good way."

She smiled faintly. "It made me nervous about all the other things I'd have to tell him eventually, and I also realized…"

Cal's heart pounded quicker as he waited for her to say it. She looked down and twisted her hands in her lap. Maybe he was wrong—it wouldn't be the first time. Maybe…

She looked up at him, and when she spoke, her voice wavered. "I like you instead."

He didn't say anything in response, but a grin spread across his face. Then he pulled her into his lap and kissed her fiercely. The kiss probably wasn't his best, as he was smiling against her lips because he was so pleased, but nonetheless, he was kissing Rose. Holding her in his arms. She was wearing a nice outfit she'd put on for another man, but that didn't matter now.

"Wait," she mumbled against his lips, then pulled back. She was laughing and smiling, though. "You like me…like that, too? It isn't just that you want to sleep with me again?"

"No. Of course I want to sleep with you, but it's not only that."

"Even though we're roommates? It makes it extra complicated."

He shrugged. "I'm sure it'll be fine."

"You don't worry nearly as much as I do, that's for sure." She sobered further. "But back to what happened. Ray didn't take it well, and he assumed, rightly, that there was someone else. He accused me of being just another Asian woman who won't date Asian guys, like I was a traitor to my community. I think he's an MRAsian."

"What's that?"

"You know MRAs? Like that, for Asian men." She sighed. "You can look it up later. I'm not in the mood to explain. Anyway, I asked for my meal to go, got my friends to pick me up, and here I am."

He'd been elated a minute ago, but now he was concerned for her, and he understood why she'd looked so miserable when he'd arrived home.

"Rose, are you okay?" he asked, stroking her hair.

"I feel drained, but I'm okay…because you're here."

"You don't think he's going to—"

"No. And I feel safe…"

Because you're here. She didn't repeat the words, but he knew what she meant, and it filled up something inside him—though he was also pretty pissed at this Ray guy.

She kissed him again, and he clutched her against him. Slipped his hand under her shirt, and she did the same, running her hands up his chest. Her touch was so familiar, yet not quite the same as it had been in August. Or maybe he just didn't remember; he couldn't think clearly right now.

Rose. Rose. Rose.

He lifted the hem of her shirt, but she placed a hand on his wrist.

"Sorry," she said. "Not tonight. After everything that's happened in the past few hours…and I've been drinking a little… and so have you…could we wait until tomorrow?"

"Of course."

"Though maybe we could try sharing a bed again? If that's okay with you?"

He nodded.

Her pretty eyes fluttered shut. "It's been a long day. I'm ready to go to sleep."

When he picked her up, she laughed in that delightful way she had, and he smiled as he carried her to her bedroom. A little while later, she came into his room wearing only a long T-shirt, and he swallowed hard.

Damn, she looked good like that.

He gave her Shelly to hold, and they got under his covers. She snuggled up against him like it was the most natural thing in the world.

And unlike the first time they'd shared a bed, she fell asleep in his arms.

~

Rose woke up knowing exactly where she was. In Cal's bed. Against all odds, she'd fallen asleep in an unfamiliar place without any problems.

Her eyes still closed, she smiled. Last night had been a roller coaster, but she'd told him how she felt, and he seemed to feel the same way.

There was a burst of joy in her chest.

She finally opened her eyes and rolled over. Cal was still asleep. He was lying on his side, facing her, and his proximity made her warm and fuzzy. He was breathing rather loudly, in a way that might bother her if she was trying to fall asleep again, but she wasn't. She just lay awake, basking in the simple pleasure of being next to him. The large, kind man, with his long hair a mess about his face.

She reached out to smooth it, as gently as possible, but he opened his eyes.

"Hey," he said.

"I'm sorry…I didn't mean…you can go back to sleep."

He chuckled softly and pulled her close. "I'd rather spend time with you."

Her body was already responding to his touch. Moisture pooled between her thighs as he ran his hand down her back. She swallowed. "I said tomorrow, and it's tomorrow. If you're interested, that is."

"I am." He rolled them over and raised himself above her, a crooked grin on his face. The pleasure of liking someone and discovering they liked you, too…it was exhilarating.

He removed her T-shirt, and his gaze roved over her hungrily, even as he maintained that goofy smile. He dipped his head to pull the peak of one nipple between his lips, and that was enough to make her gasp. His mouth was so wet and *good*. She groaned as he suckled her other breast, thrusting her fingers into his hair.

Cal turned onto his side and kissed her mouth, slipping his hand into her panties at the same time. When she felt his rough, thick finger moving between her folds, she squeezed her legs together. His focus was all on *her*, and he looked like he wanted to gobble her up as he slid one finger inside her channel.

"Oh, God," she moaned. She was so slick for him, and he moved easily inside her.

With his other hand, he pulled her panties off and tossed them aside. Then he slid down her body, under the blankets, and set his mouth on her. There was something so sexy about seeing him beneath the blankets with his head between her legs. And the things he did with his tongue…

She squirmed against his face as pleasure built inside her, higher and higher until she turned her head to the side and cried out into the pillow. She didn't say his name, was incapable of forming even a single-syllable word, but he spoke her name in a tone she couldn't describe. Maybe like he was a bit in awe?

So was she. She'd confessed to having feelings for this man last night, and now, after sleeping peacefully in his bed all night long…

"I need you inside me," she said.

He crawled up her body, and as soon as she could reach it, she grabbed the bottom of his shirt and pulled it over his head, then made quick work of his boxers. She stroked her hand up and down his hard shaft, which only made her crave him even more. For some reason, she felt the need to say, "I haven't had sex since…"

"No? Me, neither."

Her brain struggled to process that revelation as he lowered his head and devoured her mouth.

She was nervous this time, but in a different way from how she'd been nervous before. Because this time, it meant something entirely different to her—it was like a consummation of their feelings, rather than simply lust—and OMG, what was he doing with his fingers?

She arched against him, begging with her body. Kissed him harder, ran her fingernails down his broad back.

"Cal." She could manage to say his name now, but nothing more.

And when she stroked him again, he growled into her mouth and reached out to grab a condom from the bedside table. He rolled it on, then stopped to ask. "You ready?"

She nodded, and he held himself above her as he sank into her. Her body accommodated his girth, and she felt deliciously full.

"Oh, God," she murmured as he grinned down at her. She wasn't used to a man smiling like that while he was inside her.

"It feels good?" he asked.

"You know it does."

He chuckled as he began moving, looking at her fondly. Then he partially rested his weight on top of her. "Am I too heavy?"

"No, no." She liked being caught between him and the mattress. There was certainly nowhere else she'd rather be.

She arched up to capture his lips, savoring every current of pleasure that passed through her. Their connection…it was like nothing else. With one hand, she grabbed his ass, and she could feel him smile against her lips again as his hair tickled her neck and his beard scraped her chin.

He slipped a finger into her mouth, then moved it lower, between their bodies.

It was overwhelming.

And just what she needed.

She shattered beneath him, and he came at the same time.

Time passed completely differently when Rose's naked body was intertwined with Cal's. She wasn't accustomed to this intimacy, and even though she felt boneless and sated, there was a thread of discomfort within her at, well, the comfort of it all, if that made sense.

She wasn't used to feeling relaxed when she was naked like this, wasn't used to feeling like she could tell someone anything and it would all be okay.

He lifted his head. "You know how I was going to take you out for dinner, before my phone got run over? How about we do that tonight?"

"I'm supposed to go to the cider bar with my friends…"

"Don't cancel on your friends. Tomorrow, okay?"

"Okay."

He pressed a kiss to her hair. "Mmm."

Huh. This seemed so easy, and Rose was always suspicious of easy things. They frequently weren't as simple as they appeared, though Cal was a laidback guy, something which was utterly unfamiliar to her.

What if they were too different?

He turned her around and held her from behind. He was soft and comfortable, aside from the hard ridge pressing against her lower back.

He was already hard again? Though to be fair, she had no idea how much time had passed. When she wiggled against him, he hissed out a breath.

"God," he said, "I just want to fuck you again and again. Make you come any way I can."

They weren't words of romance, but they caused a swell of joy in her chest, in addition to the dampness between her legs. Her doubts receded as she rolled on top of him and rubbed herself against his erection.

"Oh, fuck," he groaned.

Rose grinned, amazed at what she could do to him.

Yes, this was going to be a very good day.

[21]

IT WAS unusual for Rose to actually have exciting news when she saw her friends. She wasn't sure what Charlotte had told everyone, but they looked at Rose expectantly.

She glanced at the tap list. "Wait until we get our cider."

"Aw, you're no fun," Nicole teased.

Once Rose had her perry in hand, she said, "So last night, I had a date with Ray…" Hard to believe it had only been twenty-four hours ago. She told Amy, Nicole, Charlotte, and Sierra what had happened.

"Bastard," Sierra said. "What the fuck is wrong with these men? They act like we're *their* women, like they own us. Some Asian guys were definitely hating on me when I was dating Colton. Remember those comments on the pictures from the gala?"

"Bastards, I agree," Nicole said. "We can talk about them later. Right now, I wanna get to the good part."

"The good part?" Rose asked.

"Yeah, the part where you had sex with Cal. Not that I need every detail, but you went home, told him how you felt, and you fucked, right?"

"Not until this morning, but…"

"Excellent. I'm glad you're getting some."

"Nicole!" Sierra said.

"Sorry, sorry," Nicole said. "I didn't mean to make you blush *that* much, Rose. I'm just glad it's working out for you, and you have that nice post-sex glow."

"I do?" Rose asked, horrified.

"She's kidding," Charlotte said. "You look happy, but it could just as well be due to reading a really good book or finding a really amazing ramen restaurant. It's not like you're walking around with an 'I just had good sex' vibe."

"Shhh," Rose hissed. "We're in public."

"So, where do you stand now?" Nicole asked. "You two dating?"

"We're going on a date tomorrow, yeah. I don't know what I'm supposed to call him—we haven't spoken about that—but it's good. I just, uh, feel weird talking about it."

"That's okay." Sierra paused to thank the waiter when her Brussels sprouts were delivered to the table. "We can talk about something else."

"I have news, actually." Charlotte lifted her hand, which had been under the table. There was a ring on her finger.

"OMG!" Nicole nearly bowled her over with a hug. "You're engaged?"

"Stop shrieking in my ear," Charlotte muttered, but she was smiling.

They all took turns hugging Charlotte and congratulating her, and Rose's joy for her friend wasn't at all tempered by wondering when it would be her turn.

"When are you getting married?" Amy asked.

"I don't know," Charlotte said, "but I'm sure my mother will call me three times a day until we figure it out. We've already had seven phone conversations, and it's barely been twenty-four hours since I told her the news."

"Wait, when did you get engaged?" Sierra asked. "Yesterday?"

"Yeah."

"He obviously didn't propose at a ballgame." Many years ago, Charlotte's ex-boyfriend had proposed at a baseball game, and it hadn't gone over well at all.

Charlotte snorted. "Mike knows me better than that. It was in private, of course."

"Hold on a second," Rose said. "You and Mike rescued me from my date yesterday. Was that before or after he proposed?"

"Not long after."

Rose's eyes widened. "Charlotte! You didn't have to come. I could have asked someone else. I just chose you because you were closest but—"

"Don't worry about it." Charlotte waved it off and took a sip of her bone-dry cider.

"Do you know who you're talking to?"

"Yeah, yeah. I know. That's why I didn't tell you yesterday—I knew you'd feel too guilty. But it's not often I get a desperate text from you, so I wasn't going to ignore it."

Rose hugged Charlotte again. "You're the bestest."

"Alright, alright, enough with the emotional display." Just as Charlotte said that, her phone rang, and she declined the call. "I told my mom I wouldn't pick up if she called again tonight. I'm not surprised she's testing me. I really should have gotten engaged *before* she retired. We've already talked for a full hour about flowers—I guess she's watched multiple floral design shows recently. Who knew there was more than one?"

"You know what you should do," said one of the servers—Julie, Charlotte's sister—as she stopped by their table. "You should threaten to elope if she interferes too much."

"Good idea," Charlotte said.

"Any time." Julie headed off to deliver a round of drinks.

"Speaking of family," Nicole said. "My grandmother has discovered house-hunting shows and spends even more time yelling at the TV now, according to Kelsey. You know how David and I are looking at buying a place together? Po Po keeps trying to give us questionable advice. Her latest video on TikTok..."

Rose's phone vibrated, and she pulled it out of her purse. Nearly everyone who'd text her was here, which meant it was probably Cal.

Hey, babe. Enjoying your evening? he asked.

She knew she must have a goofy expression on her face as she typed a quick reply. This was what she wanted: someone who'd text her when she was out, who'd think of her when she wasn't there.

"You can head home if you like," Sierra said.

Rose jumped. "What?"

"Go. Spend time with your guy."

"He insisted I see my friends tonight, as I'd planned, and I don't want to ditch you all because I'm in a new relationship—"

"You won't forget about us," Sierra said. "I trust you. But we all know what it's like at the very beginning."

"It's true," Amy said.

Rose finished her cider and considered it. "One more drink and then I'll leave."

"I bet she's gonna chug it," Nicole stage-whispered to Amy.

"Very funny." Rose shot them a mock glare.

She was delighted that it was her turn to be teased about her love life.

At ten o'clock, Rose went home and headed straight to Cal's bed. They had sex, and he fell asleep shortly thereafter, but unlike last night, she didn't fall asleep quickly.

She tried to remain upbeat. She'd lie here and eventually get some shut-eye.

However, by two o'clock, her mind had worked itself into a frenzy.

She was hugging Shelly, and she'd moved her white-noise machine into Cal's room earlier, so the sleeping conditions were pretty good. And she'd generally been sleeping well lately—it had been a couple of weeks since she'd gotten less than six hours a night. Not that she'd fallen asleep instantly all those evenings, but it had always been faster than this.

What if she was just bad at sharing a bed with someone, and last night had simply been an aberration? Wouldn't that put a damper on a relationship? Was it something she'd get better at over time? If so, how long would it take? A week? A month?

And how bad would her sleep be during that adjustment period?

Bad sleep was terrible for Rose's mood. When she couldn't sleep, she got worked up, and things just snowballed from there. She'd been improving as summer approached; she couldn't afford to slide backward.

She was usually better at making sure her brain didn't get too out of control, but it was hard when it was related to an unfamiliar thing: a relationship. Earlier, she'd felt like things were easy. Ha! She should have known she'd be proven otherwise only a few hours later.

She took a few deep breaths and hugged Shelly tighter. Nothing would be gained from lying here, wide awake. She ought to go back to her room. It felt like admitting defeat, but she needed to sleep, and that was her best shot.

Quietly, she unplugged the white-noise machine and brought it to her bedroom, along with Shelly. In her familiar bed, without someone next to her, she didn't fall asleep right away, but she managed to drift off eventually.

When Rose woke up on Sunday morning in her own bed, it was much different from when she'd woken up the day before with Cal. She wasn't well rested, and she couldn't say she was in a good mood.

She burrowed under the covers and sighed.

A few minutes later, there was a soft knock on her door, and Cal stepped inside. "Did I wake you? I was trying to be quiet in case—"

"No, no," she said, sitting up. "I was already awake."

He tilted his head and regarded her for a moment. "You look upset. Something wrong?"

"I couldn't fall asleep next to you, so in the middle of the night, I returned to my room."

"I figured that's what happened. You slept fine here, I hope?"

She nodded. "But how can I have a relationship when I can't even share a bed?"

"Would it help if the bed was bigger? Do I take up too much room? Do you like being able to spread out when you sleep?"

"No, it's not any of that."

"Well, if you can't share a bed with me, that's okay. You can sleep here when you like. No big deal." He sat down beside her and put an arm around her.

"But it's a relationship thing," she protested, "and I'm already failing at it."

"Have you had a relationship before?"

"Yeah, but not in a long time, and we didn't sleep at each other's places."

"Rose." He pulled her close. "We really don't have to share a bed at night. I don't mind. Or we can try, but please don't feel bad if you have to leave in the middle of the night. Would it be better if we slept together in your room?"

She shook her head. "I'd prefer to know I can come here and be alone."

"No problem."

"Are you sure?"

He shrugged. "Why not?"

Why not? Because not sharing a bed was a sign of a failing marriage, and they weren't even married. They'd been together for all of a day.

This relationship business was wreaking havoc on her brain.

Cal, on the other hand…

"How are you so chill?" she asked. Practically demanded.

He shrugged again, but then he said, "I was hardly 'chill' when you went on dates with Ray."

"Really?" she said. "I never noticed."

"Why do you think I was drinking on Friday night?"

"Just for fun, because you were out with your friend—*Oh*. Are you serious? You like me that much?"

"Of course. I like you a lot, and it's fine if we can't share a bed most nights. It might be awkward during the week anyway because we don't wake up and go to bed at the same time."

Right. He usually went to bed before her and got up before her.

Normally, if you'd just started dating someone, you wouldn't be living together, so you wouldn't be spending every night in the same house anyway. Their situation was a bit weird, and she started to freak out again that this was a bad idea and it wouldn't work out.

But then he lay down beside her and wrapped his arms around her, and her brain quieted.

"This way," he said, "I can sneak into your room on the weekends and feel naughty."

She chuckled as she marveled that he really did seem okay with this. She didn't think he was just pretending—that didn't seem like Cal, even if he'd pretended her dates with Ray didn't affect him. This was different.

How are you so wonderful? she nearly asked.

She settled against his bulk and rested her head on his chest, her arm across his soft stomach. He was incredibly comfy. And he wanted to be with her! It made her giddy, and she laughed.

"What's up?" Cal asked.

"Oh, nothing. Just…happy."

Just happy. Even though it wasn't *just* anything.

"Where do you want to go on our date tonight?" he asked.

"There's a Syrian restaurant I've been meaning to try. Is that okay with you?"

"Sure."

She squeezed him tight. Wow. Having a boyfriend really was awesome. It felt almost too good to be true.

She pushed aside the fear that it couldn't last. She wouldn't let her brain get to her now.

"Ooh, you know what we should do?" she said.

"What?"

"We should announce our relationship on Instagram. By which I mean, Shelly and Fred should announce their relationship. Not that we have to, but everyone's been teasing us. Them. You know what I mean."

Cal didn't say she was a weirdo. Instead, they debated for a long time—well, five minutes—where Fred and Shelly should be positioned, eventually settling on them sharing a cup of coffee downstairs. Rose posted the photo on Fred's Instagram as she ate breakfast.

Fred the Alpaca: *Life is grand when you're in love with your best friend.*

Merry Lamb: *OMG, I knew it!*

Fabulous the Unicorn: *Isn't this FABULOUS?*

Penguin Pip: *Does this mean your humans are in love too?*

Fred the Alpaca: *Yes*

However, Rose immediately regretted Fred's comments. Her alpaca had used the word "love," and it seemed a little soon for that, even if it was just their plushies talking on Instagram.

Seriously, how did Cal not think she was too weird?

But he didn't. No, he brought Shelly and Fred out to the living room, where he put them under the throw blanket together. He drew hearts on a piece of paper, colored them in with red pen, and placed them above the animals' heads on the couch before taking a picture.

Yes, he was being as weird as she was, and it was delightful.

Penguin Pip: *Aww, you're so cute together. Look at your happy smiles.*

Fred the Alpaca: *I'm always smiling. My face is stuck that way.*

Shelly the Turtle: *I think you look handsome.*

Even though it was just Cal's turtle telling her alpaca that he looked handsome, Rose glowed as if Cal had told her that she was the most beautiful woman ever.

Well, in truth, Rose might not glow if he said that. She'd have trouble believing it.

So maybe it was better this way.

Despite her earlier insistence that she wouldn't let her brain get to her, doubts started to crowd her head again. But then Cal slipped his hands under her shirt, and her fears vanished.

That evening, Rose and Cal walked hand in hand to the restaurant of her choosing.

They started with mutabal, an eggplant dip. For her main course, she tried fatteh: chickpeas and toasted pita covered in tahini-yogurt sauce and other things. He ordered something similar to hers, but it also had ground beef.

"Do you like it?" she asked after his first few bites. She hoped Cal was enjoying himself as much as she was.

"Yeah, it's kinda like nachos." He grinned at her—she would never tire of his smile—and offered her a bite.

Their date was, of course, miles better than her Friday night date with Ray, and she felt relaxed as they talked about their travels and other things. The food was all amazing, and she was pleased she could appreciate it. When her brain was at its worst, she couldn't enjoy things like good food. She was happy...and happy that she could feel happy.

For dessert, they had something similar to baklava, and when Cal reached out to swipe some syrup off her lip, she practically shuddered.

They went home and had sex before she returned to her own bed.

And this time, sleeping alone didn't make her doubt their relationship.

[22]

Monday after work, Rose was in a good mood. She and Cal would stay in tonight. He'd make dinner—he was currently at the grocery store getting ingredients—and then they'd start a new drama.

She was about to do some vacuuming when someone knocked on the door. As a general rule, she didn't answer the door for unexpected visitors, and if Cal had forgotten his keys, he'd text her. So, she didn't answer.

But then the person pounded on the door again, and Rose felt a frisson of fear skate up her spine. Tentatively, she walked to the front door and looked out the peephole. There was a white teenage girl on the porch, and she shouted something that sounded like, "Uncle Cal!"

Rose slowly opened the door. "Hello?"

The girl frowned. "Are you my uncle's roommate?"

"Yes."

"My mom and I thought he lied about you being *just* a roommate." The girl looked at Rose expectantly.

Rose didn't offer any confirmation. She felt uneasy that Cal had insisted the two of them weren't together—but that was probably before they'd hooked up again. She wasn't sure what he'd prefer to say now, and she reminded herself that if he wanted to keep their relationship a secret from his family for a little while, it was fine. It didn't mean he was embarrassed by her. Sometimes telling your family about your personal life was complicated.

"Yes," she said, "well…"

"You're definitely together," Kendall said. "Wait until I tell her… Oh, *wait*. I can't. I'm mad at her. That's why I ran away."

Rose's head was spinning. Her boyfriend-slash-roommate's runaway teenage niece was on their doorstep. She wasn't sure what to do, and being stuck in an unfamiliar situation made her anxious.

Come on, brain. Get out some words.

"Cal will be back soon." Her voice sounded a bit weird. "Why don't you come inside and wait? I'll text him and let him know you're here."

The girl seemed to think this was acceptable. "I'm Kendall."

"I'm Rose."

God, she was so not prepared to meet Cal's family. This shouldn't happen when you'd been dating for all of three days. Rose might not be an expert on relationships, but she knew that much.

"Are you hungry?" she asked. "Do you want something to drink? There's orange juice and water, or I can make tea."

"Juice is good. Thanks. Where does Uncle Cal keep his snacks? He always has the best snack food."

"Uh, I'm not sure what he has now, but you can have these, if you like." Rose took out a bag of Turtle Chips.

Kendall snapped a picture and did…Rose wasn't sure what with it. There was probably some kind of social media that she was too old and uncool to know about.

Much to her relief, Cal returned five minutes later.

"You met Rose, I see," he said to Kendall as he put away the groceries. "Wanna tell me what happened with your mom?"

This was part of why Rose didn't feel capable of dealing with the situation: she remembered being a teenage girl, and it had royally sucked. She recalled the fights she'd had with her own mother. She'd felt like she was the foolish girl who'd understand her mom's side when she was older, but as it turned out, age had made her think her mom had screwed up even more.

Sometimes parents didn't have their child's best interests at heart, and other times they did, but they expressed it in bone-headed ways or lacked the knowledge to deal with it.

Her teenage years had been a time of helplessness. Rose had known there was something wrong with her—her struggles with mental illness had started when she was fourteen—but she hadn't been allowed to get help.

Other teenagers dealt with different issues. Some had parents who didn't approve of them being queer, for example. Lying to your parents could be necessary for survival.

Rose had no idea what the situation was here until Kendall said, "I used a fake ID to go to a concert. I told my mom I was just sleeping over at Destiny's, but then my mom called Destiny's mom and realized I wasn't there."

Rose's brain stopped fully processing words, as it sometimes did. She was just thankful none of this suggested that Kendall's mom was seriously problematic.

Cal was sitting beside her at the kitchen table. She wanted to reach out and touch his knee, but she held herself back. She wouldn't give Kendall any reason to be even more certain they were together, not until she knew what Cal wished to tell his family.

"Let me see this fake ID." He held out his hand, and Rose's brain re-entered the conversation.

"Mom confiscated it, but I have a picture." Kendall showed him on her phone.

He chuckled as he shook his head. "I can't believe this worked and you actually got into the concert. Even *I* can tell this is fake."

"I'm mature for my age. That's what Dom says."

"Dom?" Cal was no longer chuckling. No, he sounded concerned.

Kendall hadn't said much, but Rose, too, had a bad feeling about this guy. Having a boyfriend in her class would be one thing, but this sounded like…

"An older guy," Kendall said.

"How old?" Cal asked.

"Twenty."

"Is he your boyfriend?"

"Not exactly, but…"

"Where did you meet him?"

"At a party."

This wasn't at all like Rose's high school experience. She and her friends hadn't been popular enough to be invited to parties, but she hadn't minded.

"I don't think you should see him anymore." Cal was clearly trying his best to sound stern, but it didn't come naturally to him.

"I thought you'd be on my side!" Kendall cried. "You're usually so much more reasonable than Mom. How can you say this stuff when you don't know anything about him?"

Cal scrubbed a hand over his beard, looking at a loss for words.

"He's, what, five years old than you?" Rose figured she'd try her best. "He's saying you're mature because he knows it's what you want to hear. He goes after girls who are still in high school because then he's the cool older guy, and he can get away with treating you like crap since you don't know anything else."

"Is that what happened to you?" Kendall asked.

"No, but to people I know."

"Dom's not like that. Besides, Mom and Dad are four years

apart, and you two…" Kendall looked pointedly at Rose's hand, which was interlocked with Cal's hand on the table.

Oops. Rose hadn't noticed that he'd reached for her hand. They immediately separated.

"Come on," Kendall said. "Don't try to pretend."

"She's six years older than me," Cal said, "but six years is different at our age. I'm not close to being underage."

Kendall looked skeptical, and she was just opening her mouth when Cal's phone rang.

He answered it. "Hi, Jodi… Yes… Yes, she told me… Okay, but she can stay here tonight if she likes… Wait." He pulled the phone away from his ear and looked at Rose.

Rose nodded.

"Yeah, it's fine…" he said into the phone. "I'll drive her home on the way to work tomorrow… Yeah, yeah. I promise…"

Kendall rolled her eyes but didn't say anything.

He ended the call. "Can you help me with dinner, Kendall? I told Rose I'd cook tonight."

This wasn't the Monday night that Cal had intended. He'd planned to cook dinner for Rose, followed by starting the new drama they'd talked about, and then, well, sex sounded good.

But having sex seemed weird when his niece was in the spare room.

It was cool that this place had an actual spare room, even if it was tiny. At his last apartment, when Kendall had come by, she'd slept on the couch. Or he'd slept on the couch and she'd slept in the bed. But here, Rose had said that as long as her dad wasn't visiting and she had some notice, he was free to have a guest make use of the extra room.

Rose hadn't exactly been given a lot of notice tonight, but she'd seemed okay with everything so far, and he was thankful for what she'd told Kendall about this Dom person. Cal hadn't known how to put it into words—he'd just known it was a bad idea.

But Kendall had listened to Rose…he hoped?

Rose would return to her bed later, but for now, she was in his bed, cuddled up against his side.

"I'm sure you didn't plan to meet my family that quickly," he said. "Sorry about that. Every few months, Kendall stays with me for a night. It helps her and Jodi cool off."

She shifted against him. "You must have been quite young when she was born."

"Yeah, my sister's a lot older than me. When she had Kendall, I was only fourteen. Kendall's a nice kid who doesn't always make the best decisions, but I know what that's like."

"My teenage years were mostly me trying to hide my mental illness and my mom getting mad at me for not being good at hiding it. She refused to let me get help."

"And your dad?"

"He mostly stayed out of it," Rose said. "One time, I heard them arguing about me, and he said I should go to the doctor… but that was all. I guess he lost that argument, because I never heard about it again. I know he thought they should be a united front with their kids, and I suspect he was still a little uncomfortable with me seeing doctors for that sort of thing. We had an argument about it a few years ago, and he was very sorry that he hadn't done more for me."

Cal waited for her to say something further about her mom, but she didn't.

And that was when he knew. Her mother must have passed away, but Rose hadn't mentioned it, and he wouldn't push her.

"My dad just got mad at me all the time for being stupid," he said, figuring she'd like a change of topic. "He still does, but it was worse when I was a kid."

"Cal—"

"It's no big deal. I grew up okay, got a job, mostly function as an adult. It's fine."

"It's not *fine*. He shouldn't have done that."

"I know it was hard for him to believe I was actually his son. But thanks to you, I know there's a name for my problem with numbers. Not that it was *only* numbers, but those were the worst."

"Hey," she said softly. "I like you as you are, and you're pretty great at lots of things."

Yeah, she'd always made him feel as if he was okay.

Cal couldn't voice everything he was feeling right now. Instead, he rolled on top of Rose and kissed her, since that seemed like the best way to express himself. He didn't intend to have sex tonight, but Kendall was on another floor, and when Rose released one of her quiet little moans, that was it. He was a goner.

It was a long time before she went back to her room to sleep.

"So you're sure that Friday works for you?" Cal's mom asked.

"Yep," he said into his phone as he walked down Bloor. "All good."

"I was thinking—"

"Mom, I'm really sorry, but I've got to go." He'd been trying to make this conversation short, but that didn't always work with his mother.

He paused outside the pub as they said their goodbyes, then slid his phone into his pocket. He wasn't looking forward to his parents coming over, but he could think about that later.

As he stepped inside, he recalled the last time he'd been here. With Rose.

"Looks like someone moved on from baking cookies to sex," Marv said when Cal sat down.

"Yeah, man," Levi said. "You're getting some? Is it your roommate?"

Cal shrugged, but that probably just confirmed what they thought.

Marv held up his hand for a high-five, which Cal slapped, though it made him feel like an immature teenager.

Levi, on the other hand, narrowed his gaze. "Aren't you afraid of what's gonna happen?"

"You mean because she's my roommate?" Cal asked.

"Yeah. Seems like a disaster waiting to happen."

"What about the other guy she was dating?" Marv asked.

"He's out of the picture." Strange to think that her date with Ray had only been a week ago. Fortunately, the bastard hadn't made any attempt to contact her since, and Rose didn't seem inclined to talk about him.

"Maybe he is," Levi said, "but what about when she, I don't know, dumps you for your cousin, or decides you're not serious enough, or is suspicious of you having female friends?"

"I don't see any of that happening." Even though they'd all happened to Cal in the past.

"Because you never do, and if she's your roommate, it'll be an even bigger mess than usual. One of you will have to move out."

"It'll be me," Cal said instantly, even though he wasn't sure how he'd afford it. "I couldn't make her leave."

"You have to think of the consequences, that's all I'm saying. Because we know you don't always do that."

Marv gave Levi a look. "And what's he supposed to do now?"

"Well, it's a little late to tell him to keep his dick in his pants, but I think that would have been the smart option."

"So he was just supposed to say nothing to the woman he really liked?"

"She's the one who revealed her feelings to me, actually," Cal said.

But even though they were talking about him, his friends didn't seem to hear him.

"He shouldn't have moved in with her in the first place," Levi said.

"Look." Cal held up his hands. "You know I didn't plan that, right? But when I saw her, I was happy to have found her again."

"You should have been thinking, *wow, this is complicated*. You should have moved out before you dated her. But once again, you weren't thinking, just like when—"

"Hey, hey," Marv said, holding a hand in each of their directions. "Can we not bring up what happened with Mia?"

Yeah, Cal might not "think" according to Levi, but he'd known where the conversation was headed.

He didn't like considering possible endings when he'd just started dating Rose. Besides, what they had was different from his past relationships, wasn't it?

He wouldn't worry about it.

$$[\ 23\ ]$$

"Ah, Rose," Dad said. "It's nice to hear from you. I haven't talked to you in a few days."

There wasn't any judgment in her father's voice about their lack of communication. He was just observing, and maybe he was a little curious. She never felt defensive with him like she had with her mother.

"I've started seeing someone," Rose said as she curled up on the couch. She figured it was okay to tell him. After all, Cal's niece knew, and as a result, Cal's sister knew.

"Is this the guy who texted when you were in Ottawa?"

"No, someone else."

"I'm happy for you," Dad said. "As long as he's treating you well?"

"He is."

"Tell me about him."

"Um," Rose said. "His name is Cal, and he's my roommate."

"Oh, the man you're living with? You're dating him now?"

"Mm-hmm."

"He's in landscaping, I remember you told me. I will drive to Toronto next weekend to meet him."

"Dad!" Rose laughed.

"You know I'm joking," he said. "But I thought I'd come to visit in a few weeks, if that's okay. Tracey's parents will be in town, and that would be a good time for me to get away for a weekend, since there will be other people here to help with the babies."

"And you want to avoid the arguing, too?"

"Ah, you remember what happened last time they visited? Yes. They have lots of strong opinions on parenting and nothing meets their approval. It's…unpleasant."

Rose thought for a moment. If her dad came, it would be impossible for him to avoid meeting Cal since they lived together, and it felt like things were moving too fast. Even though she'd met Cal's niece, meeting someone's parents seemed like a much more serious step.

Yet despite those fears, she actually *wanted* them to meet. She was excited to be dating someone as awesome as Cal, and she did want her dad to know him.

"Rose," her father said gently, "if you don't wish—"

"No, no," she said. "I do. I just have to check with him first. What are the dates you're thinking of visiting? He's away this coming weekend, but I don't think he has anything else planned after that."

Yes, Cal and his friends were going on a canoeing trip in Algonquin. He'd apologetically told her that there wouldn't be enough room for her to join, but she'd laughed and said she wouldn't want to go anyway. It sounded like a pretty hardcore canoeing trip that would involve portaging and carrying their camping gear. Rose would not be opposed to canoeing on a lake for an afternoon, but that was where her interest ended.

But as she ended the call with her father, she got caught up in her daydreams of Cal carrying a canoe towards a river. There was something attractive about him carrying, well, anything, and—

"Hey."

Rose startled as Cal sat beside her on the couch.

"Sorry," she said, "I was just daydreaming about you carrying a canoe."

He laughed. "Yeah? You think that's hot?"

She squeezed his bicep. "Absolutely."

"How's your dad?"

"I told him about you, and he's planning to visit in a few weeks—if that's okay with you?"

"Of course."

"You don't mind meeting him?"

"Well, it's going to happen at some point, right? Do you think he'll…like me?" Cal sounded a little unsure.

Her heart melted. "I'm pretty sure he'll like you just fine."

"If you think of any tips for me, just let me know. Like, what I should or shouldn't say, that sort of thing. I wanna make a good impression." He smiled. "You ready to start that K-drama?"

"Yep, let's do it," she said, picking up the remote.

The show began in the past. Rose got nervous when she started a new show—sometimes it was a lot of effort for her to figure out what was going on, but she thought she had a handle on this, more or less.

Although Cal was a little distracting. She lay on the couch with her head on his lap, and he stroked her side. It seemed like he was just touching her absently, but every caress made her smile on the inside. Yeah, she really did like being in a relationship.

But then, on-screen, a woman hanged herself from a tree.

Something was wrong. That much was obvious to Cal.

Rose was fumbling with the remote, but she couldn't seem to make it work. He gently took it from her and exited the show, a sickening feeling in his chest. His intuition told him what had happened to her mother. He wasn't entirely sure he was correct, but...

Rose sat up and tucked her head against his shoulder. She didn't say anything for several minutes, and he stayed silent, too. Just held her close and ran his hand through her hair.

"Usually, I google TV shows to see if there's suicide," she said at last, her voice a little hoarse. "But I didn't this time...and sometimes it doesn't affect me that much, it's not like I always cry...I don't know why this time...maybe because it's an Asian woman... I don't know...I shouldn't be this sensitive...it's been years..."

"Your mother?" he asked softly.

She nodded against his shoulder.

He wanted to say everything would be okay, but her mother was gone and nothing could bring her back. He hated that Rose had gone through this.

"I was twenty-five," she said. "My mom was...not well. Her depression was worse than usual, but she wouldn't admit she was depressed. Wouldn't get help, even when I pleaded with her to do so. She didn't see depression as an illness, but a personal weakness. I was living with my parents at the time, and when I came home from work one day, there were cop cars in front of our house. As soon as I saw them, I knew what had happened."

Silent tears seeped through his T-shirt, and she was quiet for a long time.

"I'm so sorry," he said, and she nodded. He didn't know what else to say, but he would hold her. Be here for her.

"I think suicide survivors often wonder *why*, but I never did. She was sick and she couldn't stand the pain anymore; that was all the explanation I needed. She never expressed suicidal thoughts to me, but I knew exactly what it was like to want to take your own life. How unbearable your existence can feel. How thinking of ending it all...can be comforting."

That was beyond his personal experience. It was difficult for him to fully understand, but he accepted what she told him.

He hated that she knew.

"Some people might think she was selfish," Rose said, "but she was in excruciating pain. Plus, her thoughts had probably twisted everything so that she believed we were better off without her. But I don't know for sure what she believed. There was no note, no last words."

He hugged her tight, and she burrowed against him.

"My relationship with her was so complicated. In some ways, she was a wonderful mom, but in other ways, it was so fucked up. When she found out I was taking antidepressants in university, she was furious with me. She treated me like I was weak and defective, and she hated that I was 'broken' in the same way as her. After she died, I was desperate to find something that would fix me. I appreciated having my illness acknowledged by doctors and other professionals, but nothing really helped me feel less depressed. Maybe nothing would have worked for my mom, either, even if she did try to get treatment, or maybe she would have been different from me." Rose sniffled. "I still think of the what-ifs sometimes. It's not like I beat myself up over it, but occasionally, I can't help wondering. She didn't give us any warning that she was planning to do it, but it was obvious she was severely depressed. What if we'd forced her to go to the hospital or... Ugh, I'm sorry for burdening you with this."

"I'm glad you told me," he said quietly.

"I just hate how people talk about suicide sometimes. Like, there's no compassion. That's part of the reason I try to avoid it in media."

"Are you..." He stopped, started again. "You're not suicidal now, are you?"

She didn't seem like she was, but what did he know?

"I mean, sometimes I still think of it," she said. "Like, there's a background level of suicidal thinking. To me, it's kind of normal. But in a very vague way, and I don't think about it much compared to other times in my life, though I was worse a few months ago." She covered her face with her hands. "Oh, God, what if they're right?"

"What if who's right?"

"The people who say you shouldn't be in a relationship if you're mentally ill, but since I'm always going to be this way, what they're saying is that I'll never deserve a romantic relationship. If you want to run, you should do it now. My brain is such a mess."

Cal was struggling to keep up with the leaps in this conversation, but he knew what he wanted. "I like your brain."

"You do?"

He turned her face so he could look at her. Her cheeks were wet and pink and possibly there was some snot coming out of her nose, but he was overwhelmed with his fondness for her.

"Yeah," he said. "It is a very nice and smart brain."

Oh, dear. He wished he were more…what was the word for when you were good at expressing yourself with pretty words?

Hmm.

But he did like her brain. She amazed him by figuring out things that he never could, and she was also fun, playful, and non-judgmental in ways he wasn't used to. Of course, sometimes you *should* judge people when they acted badly, but he wasn't talking about those situations.

"I'm not running," he said. "I'm lucky to be in a relationship with you."

She smiled at him, her face still tear-stained, and he was transfixed.

Later, she played Whitney Houston on repeat, and that night, to his surprise, she fell asleep in his bed. Unlike usual, he was the one who was wide awake because his brain was spinning.

He didn't like feeling helpless, but things had happened in Rose's life that could not be changed, and all he could do was plan something nice for her now.

He had a few ideas, but they'd have to wait until he came back from Algonquin.

[24]

Cal was gone, and Rose missed him.

And she was obsessing about the fact that she missed him. Should she miss someone when they'd been dating for such a short period of time? She remembered being weirded out when Ray had sent her an *I-miss-you* text. Was it strange that everything seemed a little less vibrant and she was counting down the days until Cal returned from his canoeing trip?

It wasn't her depression getting worse. It was different from that.

Being in a relationship had given her all sorts of new things to freak out about, and ever since they'd tried that K-drama—which she'd decided not to continue watching—she'd been freaking out a little extra.

Fun times.

Was she truly ready to be in a relationship if she had a breakdown from a K-drama?

And what if it blew up and she had to sort out a new living situation?

The idea of getting a new roommate or finding a new place to live was overwhelming, but heartbreak scared her more than anything. She remembered how she'd felt last summer when he didn't text her…and she'd only known him for one night at that point.

Now, she knew him so much better.

Now, she was accustomed to his stable, smiling presence in her life.

His current absence showed her just how used she'd become to having him around. She missed coming home to him. She missed snuggling him on the sofa. She missed snuggling him in bed before returning to her own room to read and sleep.

It's normal, Nicole assured her in a text. *I missed David when he went to a conference a few months ago.* But Nicole and David had been together for well over a year at that point.

Rose firmly told her brain to stop it. This was what she wanted; she was in a relationship with a kind man. She shouldn't worry so much. Maybe it would work out, maybe it wouldn't, but such was life.

Okay, that attitude was taking things a little far, but still. She should enjoy it and not obsess over what would happen if it didn't last. What was the purpose?

She imagined putting those worries in a box. The box wasn't properly sealed, but still. She was doing her best at compartmentalizing.

Cal had left for his trip on Thursday; it was now Sunday. He'd texted her a couple of times, but he'd warned her that he might not have a good signal, so she shouldn't be surprised if she didn't hear from him often.

That afternoon, she went out with Amy, Victor, and Hudson. It was a pleasant summer day, and they walked all the way to Parkdale for momos at a Tibetan restaurant. Rose had wanted to try this place for a while, and Amy was always up for trying new things. The butter chicken ones were Amy's favorite; Rose preferred the chili ones. Hudson tried to grab all of them.

Monday evening, when Rose heard the key in the lock, her

heart rate kicked up a notch—but not in a bad way. Cal was home, and she ran to the door and threw her arms around him as soon as he set down his bag. He looked like he hadn't had a proper shower in a few days, but he was handsome all the same, and just being in his arms was calming.

Yes, this relationship was worth it…right?

Saturday morning, Rose slowly became aware of a large presence in her bed. She and Cal had slept in their own rooms last night, but she was pleased to open her eyes and see him beside her now.

"Morning," he said.

He was wearing a white T-shirt and boxers, and his hair hung loose. She was so distracted by his appearance that it took her a moment to realize there was something else on the bed: a package wrapped in flowered paper. It was an odd shape, and the wrapping job wasn't professional—excessive amounts of Scotch tape had been used—but for some reason, that just made her smile more.

"Is this for me?" she asked, even though she knew the answer.

"Nah, it's for Fred."

She gave him a playful shove. Aside from Ray's flowers, she couldn't remember the last time someone had gotten her a present when it wasn't Christmas or her birthday. Her father wasn't much of a present person. Her mother, on the other hand, had bought her random stuff all the time. Clothes and jewelry. A mug with a bad engineering pun. A cute umbrella. When Rose had lost the umbrella two years ago, she'd been devastated.

"It's the start of your special day," Cal said.

"My special day?"

"Yup, I have it all planned. Sometimes I'll ask you to pick between one of two things, but you won't have to figure anything out."

He'd realized that "figuring things out" could be difficult for her. She wanted to kiss him.

And so she did.

"Don't you want to open your present?" he asked, pulling back with a smile.

"Oh, yeah, I should do that."

She picked up the package. It was soft and squishy and clearly a plushie. She tore off the paper to reveal a blue kraken with a red ribbon tied around one of its tentacles. Another tentacle held a tiny plush boat.

"Because we met at a steampunk bar," he explained. "Do you like it?"

"I love it! I'm gonna take a picture of him with Fred. 'New friends,' that's what the post will say on Instagram."

"Alright, then you can come downstairs…"

"Yeah? You don't want to make out a little first?" She whipped off her sleep shirt then felt a moment of uncertainty. Maybe she was ruining his plans, or maybe she was a frightful mess right now with her hair every which way.

But Cal looked like he wanted to devour her, in a completely different way from how the smiling kraken was devouring that boat.

When they finally got out of bed, he had to reheat the coffee, and he apologized that the peanut butter cookies were no longer warm, but she didn't care about that. She was having coffee and cookies for breakfast, and she hadn't had to make any of it herself.

He cleaned up the kitchen while she looked at stuff on her phone, and then he said, "What would you like for lunch?"

General questions like that were sometimes overwhelming for Rose, but as he'd promised, she wouldn't have to figure anything out. He gave her two options: bento box or tacos.

She chose the former. "But isn't it a little early for lunch?"

"The restaurant isn't all that close," he said. "I figure it's a nice day for a long walk, if that's okay with you?" He looked like he was eager to make her happy.

"Sounds good."

They headed out, hand in hand, and Rose was tempted to tell everyone she passed that the man next to her was the most wonderful person ever and she was so lucky, but she restrained herself and just focused on the feel of his large, callused hand around hers.

How had she thought he'd never intended to text her when he asked for her number? It wasn't at all like him to do such a thing. She supposed she hadn't known him as well back then, but she did now.

The words "I love you" came to her mind, but she didn't say them, not yet.

After lunch—during which Rose may have embarrassed herself by rambling about her love of food served in rectangular compartments—they walked back home, and Cal suggested they start a new drama. He had three picked out, and he'd read sufficient spoilers to know there weren't any suicides in them.

She'd seen two of the shows before. Although she wasn't always in the mood to try something new, she was today, so she picked the other one and they watched three episodes. She lay with her head in his lap, and she may have eaten another peanut butter cookie during the third episode.

Afterward, he gave her a second present: tea and a China-set steampunk novel called *Gunpowder Alchemy*. He told her to drink tea and read the book while he prepared dinner.

"Look at you, bossing me around," she teased.

The teasing part was apparently lost on him. "Of course, you can do whatever you want, but I know sometimes you don't like to think about what to do next—"

"No, no," she said. "It's perfect. Thank you."

She went to the reading nook on the second floor, and a few minutes later, he brought her a mug of tea. The tea was…well, honestly, he didn't have the greatest taste in tea, but that was okay. He could learn, and she was just delighted that he'd arranged all this for her.

She looked out the window as she sipped her tea, snuggling her new kraken to her chest. It really was amazing, the way that he was just so *sweet*.

Don't ruin it, brain. Don't ruin it.

It wasn't like her brain could find fault with today, though. The minor imperfection of the tea made it all the more endearing.

This, however, was followed by guilt. She didn't *need* something like this—a full day just for her. But she could do something special for him another time, right?

Finally, Rose was able to lose herself in the book, and she was a few chapters in when Cal entered the room, wearing her pink floral apron, and she smiled.

"Dinner's ready," he said.

Dinner was a big Caesar salad with grilled chicken breast, accompanied by garlic bread. She didn't know what he'd done to this bread, but honest to God, it was the best garlic bread she'd ever tasted. When she let out an admittedly exaggerated moan and licked the butter off her fingers, his easy smile disappeared, and his gaze was laser-focused on her mouth.

She assumed dinner was the end of his plans for the day, although he might have a few movies picked out.

But he surprised her by saying, "Let's go to Nautilus for a drink."

～

The very best thing in life, Cal decided, was making Rose smile. A year ago, he hadn't known this pleasure, and now he practically lived for it.

When he'd told her where they were going, she'd put on the dress she'd worn on that night back in August—there was no way he would have forgotten that dress. He had distinct memories of where the hem hit her leg, of lifting her skirt and feeling how wet she was for him.

Maybe coming here was a mistake. He was desperate to sink inside her, and now they were in public, though perhaps they could find a small washroom on one of the upper floors...

"Ooh, look, it's free!" she said as they stepped inside Nautilus.

He had no idea what she was talking about, but then she scurried toward the table under the blimp, and he understood.

The exact place where they'd first met.

"How about you get us some drinks?" she suggested. "I'll guard our table. Wouldn't want someone to steal it if I just left my cardigan." She winked.

"Yeah, that really would be too bad," he said. "You stay here and protect our table from the kraken. What do you want to drink?"

"Surprise me."

"Dangerous words."

He got them each something called "Adventurer's Punch," and when he returned to the table, Rose was positioning the stuffed kraken he'd given her earlier.

"Where did that come from?" he asked. "I didn't see you carrying it."

"Oh, it came in my purse."

He regarded her purse. It seemed like a miracle of physics that she'd been able to fit the kraken in there, but then again, what did he know about physics? He'd leave that stuff to Rose.

"I remember," he said, "that you wished you'd brought your stuffed alpaca."

She put a hand to her mouth. "Oh my God! I did say that. Worst thing to say when a cute guy tries to steal your table."

"I honestly thought someone had forgotten their sweater, and I said you could have the table, but thanks for calling me 'cute.'"

She laughed into her drink. "Mmm. This is good. But seriously, it didn't scare you off when I started talking about my stuffed alpaca?"

"Nah, I was curious."

"You were hoping I'd invite you back to my place so you could meet him?"

He laughed. "What can I say?"

"But instead, we ended up at your place."

There were a few uncomfortable seconds of silence. She was probably thinking about how he hadn't texted her, and he did feel bad about being such a klutz, but it had turned out alright in the end, hadn't it?

Once they were done their drinks, Rose led him to the top floor of the building, which appeared to be some kind of fancy English tea place. Huh. She ordered them tea that came in a dainty teapot with a pattern of roses and…gears? He wasn't quite sure. Some kind of technical thingies and flowers. Rose would probably know the details, but she was busy oohing and aahing over the baked goods that had arrived.

Yes, he was happy he'd brought her here. His hands looked like freaking bear paws around the dainty cups, but it was all good.

And he soon discovered he had a thing for women eating scones.

Okay, maybe just Rose eating a scone, after slathering it with something that she called clotted cream. He couldn't help himself from sliding his hand up her bare leg, and when her lips parted in shock, he quickly drew back.

"No, no," she said, as though she already missed his touch. "It's just…maybe…"

He enjoyed when his touch made her unable to form words. "Wanna get off behind the building again?"

Her cheeks pinkened, and she pushed her glasses up her nose.

Yep. Adorable.

"You know I can give it to you good." He slid his hand up to stroke her inner thigh.

"I…know." She squeezed her thighs together, capturing his finger between them.

He was filled with the urge to feel her tremble and clench around him, even if it had last happened only that morning. God, he needed her.

"Let's go home," she said.

Home. It was the same place for both of them, which made him smile, even if he'd have to wait a little while to touch her properly.

As soon as they were inside the house and he'd closed the front door, she dropped to her knees, a saucy look on her face. A look she hadn't worn the night they'd met, but she was more confident and comfortable with him now. She slid down the zipper of his shorts, and he scrubbed a hand over his face.

Oh, fuck.

She gave him a few strokes, until he was rock hard.

"Thanks for planning such a lovely day," she said.

"You're welcome." He thought those were the right words in this situation, but it was difficult to remember. His brain wasn't functioning.

Then she put her mouth on him.

She was still wearing her glasses, and oh God, that was hot. And the way it felt, being in her mouth, was incredible.

He slumped against the door and shoved his hands through his hair. "I won't last long."

She released him. "I know." With a little smile, she licked the underside of his cock, then took him in her mouth again.

He clenched his hands at his sides. Her mouth was so warm and wet and...

He exploded, and she continued sucking on him until she'd swallowed every last drop. That image of her licking his cum off her lips, while still on her knees and wearing her glasses... He could jerk himself off to that again and again.

"Let's go upstairs," he said. "I still gotta fuck you."

"You *just* came."

"The advantage of dating a younger man."

Inside his bedroom, he practically tore off her clothes—but he made sure he didn't ruin her pretty dress—before tugging off his own shirt. Her panties hit the floor next, and when he gently pushed her back onto the bed, she laughed.

She was certainly a sight to see. Fucking gorgeous.

It was his turn to put his mouth between her legs. He gave her one long lick.

"Cal," she said.

Oh, yes. Hearing her say his name was as good as seeing her smile.

He circled her clit in the way she liked best—he'd always known how to please her, but now, he fancied himself an expert.

She bucked her hips against him. "Please... I want..."

He gave her pussy another lick, and then he shed the rest of his clothes and rolled on a condom. She spread her legs wider, inviting him in, but he turned her onto her stomach so her ass was in the air. Oh, yeah, that was nice. He gave her ass a light smack before sinking inside her in one smooth motion. After the way he'd prepared her, she came immediately, clenching around his cock and sobbing into the pillow. It sounded like she was sobbing his name, but it was hard to tell because he was overwhelmed by the feeling of being inside her.

He slowed down after her orgasm, knowing that was what she preferred, and gradually increased his pace again. Her cries filled the room, and her hips collapsed on the bed—she was unable to hold herself up anymore.

He lowered his body and pressed kisses up and down her neck, her shoulder, barely able to think of what he was doing, only able to feel. She turned her head and pressed her mouth to his. Her kisses were desperate and sloppy, and when he came inside her, she toppled over the cliff again.

And as he held her afterward, he knew he never, ever wanted to let her go.

Cal woke up at three in the morning when Rose climbed out of bed and left the room. He wasn't sure if she was using the washroom or returning to her own room to sleep.

When she came back to his bed, he smiled. "Hey."

"Sorry, did I wake you?"

He didn't answer, just wrapped his arm around her. He knew she couldn't usually fall asleep like this, but he needed to touch her briefly.

She rolled away from him a minute later. He thought he heard tears, but he didn't know; maybe he was imagining it.

"You okay?" he murmured.

"Yeah."

But he wasn't sure she was telling the truth.

If she was upset now, he didn't think it had to do with him. They'd had a good day, and she'd said she'd enjoyed herself—Rose wasn't the sort to leave you in the dark about such things.

Cal knew he couldn't fix all her problems, no matter how much he wanted to take away her pain. And he did want to do that. Badly.

Instead of going back to sleep, he tried something he rarely did: thinking of the future.

You never think. That was what Levi had said about Cal the other week, and Cal assumed his friend had been talking about what had happened several years ago. Cal had started something with a woman in their friend group. One he knew had a crush on him; he'd known she liked him more than he liked her, and of course their relationship hadn't lasted. He'd ended it, and she'd left their group—and they didn't see her again.

But Cal wasn't twenty-two anymore, and he did think about consequences. Sometimes.

Yes, a breakup could be messy because they were roommates, but he was determined to make sure they didn't split up. Although he'd never thought a lot about having a future with someone before, he pictured him and Rose taking care of each other for years to come. Getting gray hair and creaky joints and shit like that.

He'd screwed up other things in his life, but he hoped this would be different. He was gonna do his best and pray it would all work out.

Rose's brain was freaking out again, because of course it was.

Cal was asleep now, and maybe it would be best if she went back to her own bedroom, but she foolishly wanted to stay near him, even if it made it harder to sleep.

He'd arranged such a nice day for her. He didn't seem to think the things he did were a big deal, but she'd never been in a relationship like this before.

With every day, she fell a little more in love with him. Every day, the pain she'd feel when it ended only grew.

He'd gotten her a plush kraken, and he hadn't been weirded out when she'd brought it to Nautilus. He'd made decisions for her, but not in a bossy way; rather, in an *I-want-to-ease-your-mental-load-and-make-you-happy* way.

How could she not be in love with him?

This was the supportive romantic relationship that she'd yearned for. In fact, it was even better than what her brain had been able to conjure up.

And she couldn't help feeling uneasy.

She didn't think Cal was pretending—he seemed like an open book—but his feelings could change. Something could change that would make this all go to shit.

Maybe she was catastrophizing, but look at what had happened with Ray. She hadn't seen his misogyny coming.

And with her mother…

Even though Rose had known her mother was very sick, and even though Rose had been familiar with suicidal thoughts, she'd never imagined her mother would just be…gone. She'd understood, but she'd never expected.

Sometimes the worst really did happen, and her personal experience had given her no reason to expect the best.

Was this supportive relationship an illusion? Or something that could only be temporary?

$$[\ 25\ ]$$

"DO YOU SEE WHAT I MEAN?" Rose asked, pointing to something on the spreadsheet.

Cal scrubbed his hands over his face. The numbers made even less sense than usual, and he hadn't thought that was possible.

They'd both left work slightly early today because her father was arriving soon. However, he'd been delayed, so Cal and Rose were using the time to review his monthly finances.

It wasn't going well.

"Is something wrong?" she asked, because of course she could tell.

Cal wasn't normally nervous about meeting new people, but he couldn't help worrying that Rose's dad wouldn't think Cal was good enough for her.

Which Cal understood. At times, he was amazed she was with him, but he also knew he treated her properly.

He just hoped he'd be enough for Rose's father. If Rose wasn't close to her dad and didn't value his opinion, Cal wouldn't care as much, but she talked to him several times a week, and not just because she felt obligated. Her dad was clearly important to her, and although she'd assured Cal that everything would be fine, she seemed a little anxious.

"Cal?" she said.

"Oh, you know, just a tiny bit nervous about meeting your old man. What if I tell him about the time I ate a crayon on a dare and puked afterward?" He was being a bit of a goof. He had enough control over his mouth not to say that.

"How old were you?" Rose asked.

"Uh, fifteen? Old enough to know better."

She laughed at him in an affectionate way. "We'll do this later, okay?" She gestured to the laptop. "We don't—"

Just then, there was a knock on the door.

"How about you stay here?" she said. "You don't have to come to the door. We'll wait until he sets down his bags and puts on his slippers."

Rose headed to the entrance, and Cal shut down his computer. He was suddenly hit with the odd feeling that he was forgetting something. Maybe some kind of etiquette for meeting a woman's father… No, it was something else.

"Dad," Rose said, and Cal stood up as she re-entered the room with her father. "This is my boyfriend, Cal."

Cal was momentarily stunned by hearing her say "boyfriend."

Not in a bad way—no, he quite liked it.

"Cal, this is my father. Ernest."

Cal held out his hand. "Nice to meet you." That was a safe thing to say, wasn't it?

Ernest's handshake wasn't at all threatening, no *you better not hurt my daughter or else*. Mind you, that would have been hard to pull off, seeing as Rose's father was a slight man who was at least eight inches shorter than Cal. It made Cal very conscious of his size.

There was a moment of awkward silence.

"Rose has told me all about you," Ernest said. "So I could ask what you do for work and where you grew up, but I know all the answers." He didn't speak in a menacing *I-know-all-about-you* way. It was just a statement of fact.

"You've had a long drive," Cal said. "Can I get you something to drink? Coffee, tea, wine?"

"Some wine would be nice."

"Dad!" Rose said.

"What, I cannot drink wine? I'm not driving again tonight."

"Of course you can. I just rarely see you drink."

"Well, he offered."

Cal wondered if that had been a mistake. He went to the kitchen to fetch a bottle of red wine—one that Rose had picked out because of the cute label—as well as a corkscrew since the bottle didn't have a screw top. He sat on the couch next to Rose and set about opening the bottle. His hands felt large and clumsy, but he managed to get it open without any trouble.

However, there was still something niggling at the back of his brain. Like he had something else he was supposed to do today?

"Ah, you managed that well," Ernest said. "I don't know why, but I'm always bad with corkscrews."

Rose chuckled. "Remember when you met Tracey's parents before the wedding?"

"Aiyah, don't remind me."

She turned to Cal. "Half the cork ended up floating in the bottle."

"You're making me look bad in front of your new boyfriend!" Ernest teased. Then his gaze moved to the stuffed kraken on the coffee table.

"Cal got it for me." Rose spoke like she was proud of him for getting such a thoughtful gift, but Cal wasn't entirely sure what this man would think of him buying a plush toy.

Ernest nodded. "He knows you well."

"He does."

Okay, this really wasn't going too badly. Not like any of the nightmare meet-the-parents situations in sitcoms or movies. And yes, he'd met a woman's parents before, but he hadn't cared quite so much about the outcome back then.

Yet he still couldn't banish the feeling that he was forgetting something.

"Are we going out to dinner tonight?" Ernest asked.

"No, I thought it would be easiest to stay in," Rose said. "You've had a long day. We'll go to that dim sum place you like tomorrow. Tonight, I'll make steamed fish."

"She makes it just like her mother," Ernest said. "Do you cook, Cal?"

"Yeah, but I'm no fancy chef."

"It's good to have basic skills, though."

"Yes."

"I don't mean to grill you," Ernest said.

"Sir, you're really not…"

Ernest waved this away. "I just want to make sure you can take care of her a little, okay? I don't want her to have to do all the chores, and I hear there are still men of your generation who expect that. Or they do, what is it called, weaponized incompetence?"

Rose laughed. "What are you reading?"

Cal hadn't heard of "weaponized incompetence" before and wasn't entirely sure what it meant, but it appeared nobody thought it applied to him.

Ernest just wanted to make sure Cal wasn't an asshole who didn't pull his weight, and Cal respected that. He might not have a fancy degree or job, but he didn't get the sense that was an issue—Rose had been right.

"Maybe it's good you're living together from the beginning," Ernest said. "I don't think all couples should do this, but there are things you won't learn about another person until you live together, yes?"

Cal sipped his wine and nodded as he relaxed against the

couch, but then the doorbell rang and he realized what he'd forgotten.

Shit.

Now Ernest was going to think less of him.

Cal's parents would, too, but given he'd spent his whole life failing to live up to his father's standards, that wasn't as big of a deal.

He opened the door, and sure enough, it was his mom and dad.

When Cal had spoken to his mother a few weeks ago—right before he'd met up with Levi and Marv—she'd invited herself over because she wanted to see his new place and meet the girlfriend that she'd heard about from Kendall. He hadn't remembered to put the date in his phone when he'd arrived at the pub.

Oops.

"Hey, Mom and Dad," he said with a smile. "You know, I kinda forgot about today and didn't buy enough food."

"That's okay, honey," Mom said, though she did look disappointed in him. "I'll take a peek in your cupboards. I'm sure we can find something."

Dad frowned. "You forgot?"

"Oh, well, you know how it is." Cal ran a hand through his hair.

"No, I don't know how it is to forget a visit from my own parents."

"Could we reschedule for—" Cal began.

"It's fine." Mom patted his shoulder. "We'll manage with what you have, or we'll go out."

"Rose's father is visiting from out of town."

"Then we'll meet him and Rose together. How convenient."

"No, I really think…"

Mom slipped off her shoes, ducked under his arm, and headed into the living room. "You must be Rose."

~

Rose was freaking out. What else was new?

But while she sometimes freaked out excessively, she was pretty sure it was normal to freak out when your father and your boyfriend's parents were meeting each other for the first time. Unplanned.

Rose did much better when she could mentally prepare for such situations.

She and Cal were in the kitchen, getting more wine and taking out the charcuterie platter she'd prepared earlier.

"I'm so sorry," he whispered. "It totally slipped my mind, and I suggested we reschedule, but my mom…"

His mother had looked momentarily surprised when she'd seen Rose, as if Rose hadn't been what she'd expected. Rose assumed Cal's mom hadn't been informed that his girlfriend was Asian. The woman hadn't said as much, however; instead, she'd extended a perfectly manicured hand that had made Rose feel frumpy in comparison.

"It's okay," she told Cal, even though it didn't feel okay. He'd made a mistake; everyone made mistakes on occasion. She didn't like the situation, but she couldn't be angry with him.

He hugged her. Although she knew he was a little nervous about the circumstances as well, he concentrated on her. She buried her nose in his shirt and breathed in the scent of clean laundry, focusing on the comfort of being enveloped in his arms.

Then they went out to the living room together. She gestured for Cal's parents to sit on the couch as she poured them some wine, and Cal got two chairs from the dining room table.

It was a bit hard to believe these people were Cal's parents. There was little physical resemblance, but it wasn't just that. Of course, not everyone in a family had the same personality, but still.

"So, Rose," Cal's mom said, "what do you do?"

"I'm an electrical engineer," Rose replied.

Cal's parents looked at each other, apparently surprised by this fact. Was it because she was a female engineer? There were lots of female engineers. Sure, electrical tended to be more male-dominated than some other disciplines, but...

"Really?" Cal's father said, turning to Cal. "You're dating an engineer?"

"Duncan is a structural engineering professor," his mother said, pasting on a smile.

Rose got it now. His parents hadn't expected an engineer to date someone like Cal. She thought back to some of the things he'd said when they were going through his finances, about his father's frustrations with his inability to do math.

His father didn't ask what she saw in Cal, but Rose felt like he wanted to.

"Where did you go to school?" he asked instead.

"Queen's," she answered.

"How about you?" Rose's father turned to Cal. "Where did you go to college or university?"

Oh, no. Rose didn't see this going good places.

"I figured a high school diploma was enough for me," Cal said with a laugh.

Dad nodded. "Not everyone needs a post-secondary education, and it's getting more expensive. The cost-benefit analysis..."

Rose noticed Cal's eyes glaze over at "cost-benefit analysis" but he kept smiling. A fake smile that looked rather like his mother's. Apparently, there was some resemblance after all.

"He wouldn't have had to pay for it himself," Cal's father said. "If he got in." He glanced at Rose's father with an odd expression —she couldn't help wondering if it was a *you're-Asian-aren't-you-supposed-to-be-all-for-education?* look, but perhaps she was wrong about the stereotyping.

She put down her wineglass and gripped Cal's hand. "Cal might not be book smart, but I'm very lucky to have him. He's the best boyfriend I've ever had. You raised a very kind and considerate man."

"Kind and considerate?" his father said under his breath.

Rose knew that if anyone insulted her, Cal would defend her. She *knew*, even though it hadn't happened before. But he wasn't defending himself.

His mother shot her a small smile before looking pointedly at Rose's lap.

Rose glanced down. She hadn't even noticed that she'd grabbed the kraken plushie. She was holding Cal's hand in her right hand, but with her left, she was gripping the plushie and stroking it with her thumb.

They probably thought she was childish.

They'd be horrified by the number of plushies in her bed right now.

As she sat there, surrounded by her boyfriend's parents and her father, in the house that she and her boyfriend lived in together, she started to freak out even more.

Their relationship really was serious, wasn't it?

Was she ready for this? What was she getting herself into?

They hadn't been together all that long, and they hadn't talked about their future at all. What did Cal actually want with her?

And, oh God, had she made a complete mess of this meeting? Why did she have to grab the kraken? Had it been wrong of her to stick up for Cal?

No, she couldn't regret that.

He squeezed her hand before standing up. "Look, Mom and Dad, I'm sorry, but I totally forgot you were coming today and Rose didn't expect it. How about we reschedule for another day, okay? Ernest just arrived from Ottawa. It's not the best time, and I know, it's all my fault." He shrugged with a charming grin that would probably work on most people but clearly not on his dad.

Rose had more things she wanted to say to Cal's father, but her brain failed to put the words together, and now her own dad was looking at her in concern and there was a strange noise... Was that the doorbell?

Yes, definitely the doorbell, ringing over and over.

Cal stalked to the door, and when she heard a commotion, she joined, followed by her father and Cal's parents.

Ray leaned heavily on the doorframe. He'd always looked polished before, but today, he was clearly drunk.

"What are you doing here?" Cal demanded. "Ray, right? She doesn't want to see you anymore. Can't you get that through your thick skull? If you show up here again, I'll break your fucking nose."

Ray looked like he was going to say something stupid, but then Rose's father, who had to be half Cal's weight, got in Ray's personal space, and whatever look he gave Ray seemed to scare Ray more than anything. He scampered down to the sidewalk and tripped on the curb, and Rose shouldn't laugh, but she did.

"Who was that?" Cal's mom asked.

"Uh, I went on a few dates with him," Rose said, "but he turned out to be a jerk."

Cal wrapped his arms solidly around her middle. Come to think of it, her legs did feel like jelly and were on the verge of giving out, but he'd realized that before she did.

"You okay?" he murmured.

No, she wasn't. She was embarrassed and overwhelmed.

Distantly, she became aware of Cal's parents leaving, and she might have mumbled a goodbye, maybe not.

Oh, God. Was she making a mess of things?

[26]

"I LIKE HIM," Dad said, patting Rose's knee. They were sitting together on the couch.

"Yeah?" She didn't know why there was so much surprise in her voice. She'd expected that he and Cal would get along.

"I'm not so sure about his parents," Dad continued, and Rose managed a weak laugh. "But I can get along with them for the wedding."

"Dad!"

"Ah, sorry. I shouldn't make jokes about that yet. I'm just glad you're happy with him."

Rose glanced toward the kitchen. In the aftermath of what had happened, Cal had volunteered to cook dinner instead of Rose, so she'd save the fish for tomorrow.

"It's not like I can depend on another person for my happiness," she said to her father.

"No, but he makes everything a little better, doesn't he? I can see how you look at him."

"Except he forgot about his parents visiting. Which is okay, it happens, but why couldn't I have managed better? And then Ray showed up."

"You're doing fine." He rubbed her back. "Don't be so hard on yourself."

She rested her head on his shoulder. "You know it's not that simple."

He kept rubbing her back in a soothing motion. He'd always been affectionate with his children, something that had surprised Sierra when Rose had told her.

"I wish Mom could have met him," she said suddenly.

"I know. She would have liked him."

"Are you sure?"

"Yes, because he's good to you. She would have understood that, even if she didn't understand other things. I'm sorry, Rose."

I'm sorry she couldn't accept that she was sick, and so were you. I'm sorry I didn't do more to get you help when you were young.

He didn't say those words, but Rose knew what he meant. They'd had enough conversations about it before.

That night, she decided to try sleeping in Cal's bed, but if she couldn't fall asleep, she'd go back to her bed in an hour, and she reminded herself that this was okay.

Her mind was much less serene about other things, however.

"Again, I'm so sorry about my parents," Cal said.

"Ugh, what must they think of me?" Rose burrowed against him. "A guy I used to date showed up drunk, and I basically had a meltdown."

"And you defended me. I'm not used to people defending me to my parents."

"I hope I didn't make things complicated."

"Don't worry," he said. "I'm not that close to them. You were perfect."

"Ha. I'm hardly perfect."

"To me you are."

For a split second, she thought she might cry.

～

The rest of her father's visit went better.

On Saturday morning, Rose woke up in her own bed, cuddling Fred to her chest, and when she went downstairs, her father and Cal were drinking coffee and talking about gardening. She'd told Cal that he didn't need to entertain her father like this, but Cal didn't seem to mind, and truth be told, she was glad to see the two most important men in her life getting along.

They all went out for dim sum together, and afterward, Cal headed home while Rose and her father walked around the city and had tea. For dinner, she made the steamed fish that she'd intended to make on Friday.

All in all, it went quite well, and it made her love Cal even more. True, her father was a reasonably easy man to like, but still. She felt as if she must be dreaming, and Cal would turn out to be a serial killer or alien in disguise. Yes, those seemed far-fetched, but they seemed more likely than suddenly finding herself in a solid relationship after all this time.

When her father left on Sunday afternoon, Rose was about to do some cleaning when she got a text from Amy. Amy had a headache and wondered if Rose could look after Hudson for a couple of hours until Victor got home. Happy to spend some time with a cute baby, Rose agreed, and Cal volunteered to go with her.

"I mean, if Amy wouldn't mind," he said.

"I'm sure she wouldn't."

Amy really didn't seem well when she opened the door. She was normally perky, but today she looked exhausted and bedraggled, and Rose's chest squeezed with worry.

"The headache is pretty bad, and the painkillers don't seem to be working." Amy passed the baby to Rose. "I just fed him. I'm going upstairs to take a nap."

Rose and Cal sat on the couch in the front room. Hudson regarded Cal curiously and reached for his beard.

"Hey, little guy," Cal said. "What's your name?"

"Bababa," Hudson said.

"Okay, I'll call you Bababa."

Hudson giggled. Since they were getting along, Rose handed Hudson to Cal.

Cal stood the baby up on his feet. "Aren't you a handsome little Bababa?"

In response, Hudson tried to smush Cal's nose with his tiny hand.

If Rose and Cal had a baby, perhaps they'd look like Hudson— one white parent, one East Asian parent. But she couldn't give that to him. It was possible he didn't want kids, but when she looked at him playing with Hudson, she couldn't believe that. She thought of him with his teenage niece, too. He'd be a good parent —he would be way more understanding than his own father.

What if...?

No. She'd known for years that having small children wasn't a possibility for her. It wasn't safe. Why, just look at Amy, who was way more equipped to handle a baby and looked like a mess today.

"Ga," Hudson said.

"Ga," Cal repeated.

"Ah."

"Ah."

Rose figured this would amuse both of them for a while.

But Cal's attention wasn't all on Hudson, because a minute later, he said to Rose, "Are you okay, hun?"

No, she wasn't. She was a ball of anxiety. All of her concerns about their relationship were hitting her at once. Consuming her.

She couldn't keep doing this. Everyone had issues, but he deserved someone who didn't have quite as many issues as she did. He was better off without her.

When he touched her leg, she stiffened.

"Rose?" he said as he returned his hand to Hudson, who was attempting to blow raspberries. It was adorable, and it made her heart hurt.

She couldn't imagine Cal saw their future the same way as she did. Yes, she didn't know exactly what he wanted, but she doubted it was the same thing. And although he was easygoing, he'd eventually get frustrated with her.

"What *is* his name?" Cal asked.

"Hudson."

"Hudson, why don't you go cheer up Rose?" Cal handed over the baby.

Oh, God.

I will not cry. I will not cry. I will not cry.

"Mamamama," Hudson said.

He was just babbling. It didn't mean anything. But it was getting harder and harder for Rose to maintain her composure.

She hugged him close and squeezed her eyes shut to stem the tears. And when he slapped a sticky hand against her cheek and nearly poked out her eye, she just wanted to cry harder—and not because it physically hurt.

She couldn't look at Cal. Couldn't bear to see his expression of concern. Couldn't bear to think about how she had to put an end to this as soon as possible, before it could break her heart even more.

Thankfully, Victor arrived home earlier than expected. Rose didn't try to make conversation with him—Victor probably wouldn't care for small talk anyway—and headed next door as quickly as possible, Cal following.

"Babe, talk to me," he said. "What's up? I can tell something's wrong."

She took her time removing her shoes in the entryway, stalling.

It was the right thing to do for both of them. She knew that.

But they lived together and this was going to be such a mess and the past few weeks had been so amazing and she was going to miss him so much and…

"I think we should break up," she said.

$$[\ 27 \ ]$$

Cal led Rose to the couch. They both sat down, and he took her hand.

"What did I do wrong?" he asked. He must have screwed up somehow.

"Nothing," she said.

"Then…why? I love you, Rose."

That just made her cry.

"Come on, whatever it is, I'll fix it, I promise." He wasn't used to feeling this desperate.

"Being in a relationship has just given me more things to worry about."

"Tell me, and I'll tell you why you don't have to worry." Maybe that was wishful thinking on his part, but he would do his best, whatever it took.

"What do you think about our future together?" she asked.

"I haven't thought about the details, but I know I really want to be with you."

"You're sure?"

"Yeah, you're great, Rose."

She shook her head. "You don't think me getting anxious and depressed is too much to deal with?"

"Nah, it's all good."

"You know there will be times when I'm sicker than I am now."

"Yeah, and we'll manage." He didn't like the idea of her being unwell, of course, and he couldn't solve everything, but he could take care of her.

"My family history doesn't bother you?"

"I don't like that you had to go through it, but no. If you get really sick…we'll find a way to keep you safe."

She looked away.

"Tell me what else is going on," he said, pulling her closer.

When she still didn't speak, he handed her the kraken, and she stroked its softness.

"I don't want to have kids," she said.

"Okay."

"Just 'okay'?"

"Yeah, if you don't want to have kids, we won't have kids." He shrugged. "No big deal."

"It's not 'no big deal.' It's one of the most important decisions you make in adulthood. Do you see yourself having kids?"

"It's occurred to me before, but I've never thought about it a lot, so I guess it's not important to me. You're important to me, Rose." He didn't have the words to express how much she meant to him. "I'm happy without kids."

"The idea of getting pregnant and giving birth and caring for a newborn…it freaks me out more than anything, which is saying a lot." She paused and looked down at the kraken. "One of my sisters-in-law had such a terrible pregnancy. Couldn't keep food down, had to be on bedrest. She'd wanted to have two kids, but she decided she couldn't go through it again. I know myself, and I couldn't handle that sort of thing well. And even if the pregnancy was okay, caring for a baby would be the worst thing for my depression, especially because it would wreak havoc on my sleep. I have no desire to go through any of it. And toddlers who have no sense of self-preservation and can't properly express themselves—I wouldn't want to be responsible for one."

He nodded. "I get it."

"There's a small chance I'd be interested in adopting older kids one day, but would I even be able to adopt with my history of mental illness, when it's so treatment resistant and my meds don't do a lot? I don't know. I'm not sure yet if I'd want that—and it would have to be the best thing for the kids—but I know there are some things I don't want. A baby is one of them."

"Okay."

"You're not going to try to convince me that I'm wrong? That I could do it? It's not that I think nobody with mental illness should have a baby, but for me, personally…"

"You don't want it," he said, "so why would I try? You know yourself better than I know you, and I trust you to know what's best."

"Sometimes I'm a bit torn because I do love babies. When they smile at you, there's no better feeling. But as soon as I start thinking about having my own, I get terrified."

"I could have—what's it called? A vasectomy? Do those hurt a lot?"

"You might need a bag of frozen peas on your balls for a weekend, but they're not supposed to be that bad. Less invasive than me getting my tubes tied. I could go on birth control pills again, though I prefer not to because they weren't good for my mood. Maybe I should look into getting an IUD…"

"I'll get a vasectomy," he said.

"You're making the decision just like that?"

"Why not? You change your mind about breaking up?"

⁓

No, Rose hadn't changed her mind, although she felt a glimmer of hope.

Maybe it really could be this easy after all?

How was her boyfriend so awesome and reassuring? How had she happened to find a guy who was cool with not having kids?

She shouldn't have immediately assumed he wanted a baby because he was good with Hudson. She liked babies, too, as she'd told him, but that didn't mean she wanted to be the mother of one.

She looked at Cal. "Can I ask you another question?"

"Sure," he said.

"Have you had many relationships before?"

"A few."

"Did you end them, or did the other person end them?"

"Sometimes her, sometimes me."

She fiddled with the tag on her kraken. "How did you fall out of love?"

"Most of the times, I wasn't really in love. Not like I am with you."

Coming from someone else, Rose might have brushed that off —there were smooth guys who'd say anything to get in someone's pants—but she felt confident now that Cal wasn't like that at all. He wasn't a super serious guy, but he was always sincere. Straightforward.

She loved that about him.

And she was starting to believe they had a future together, and even if terrible things had happened to her in the past, good things could happen to her, too. It didn't mean she was dreaming. Or foolish and naïve.

It was all possible.

"Okay," she said. "I believe you and I'll try to stop worrying so much. I can't promise I won't worry at all, of course, since my brain always leaps to new worries."

"The leaps your mind makes...they amaze me."

She gave him an affectionate slap on the shoulder.

He smiled at her hesitantly. "Have you changed—"

"Yes," she interrupted. It was a bit of a risk, but it was worth it. "Yes, I've changed my mind and I want to stay with you and build a life together, one that doesn't involve having a baby or sharing a bed all the time..."

She lost the ability to form words when she saw the grin on his face. Although she might not have much relationship experience, despite being thirty-five, she couldn't say she minded. She was here now, and she had a great guy who was looking at her in such a sweet way as he wrapped his arms around her...

Ooh, those really were some nice biceps.

"You feelin' me up?" he asked.

"Maybe a little," she said. "You mind?"

"Of course not."

"I'm glad you tried to steal my seat at Nautilus. Although if we'd ended up being roommates without that meeting, maybe it would have still turned out the same."

Except she wouldn't have been crestfallen when he didn't call her. Still, she couldn't wish she hadn't met him back then because she was happy with everything now. Very happy, even if she'd continue to have small relationship-related worries.

As she burrowed against him and pressed her face into the crook of his neck, she felt...safe. He couldn't protect her from everything, but it was so nice to have him beside her.

"I love you," she murmured.

"I love you, too."

She tilted her head up and was about to kiss him when the doorbell rang.

"That better not be Ray again," Cal said.

Rose didn't think Ray would come back, but if he did, she'd have to figure out her options. She'd already blocked his number, and he hadn't tried to contact her under a different one. She didn't have any social media accounts under her real name, but she was lucky he hadn't done some sleuthing and harassed her online. She'd heard some terrible stories.

Not sure what to expect, she followed Cal to the door. Charlotte stood on the porch carrying a take-out cup of coffee.

"Hey," Cal said. "Charlotte, right?"

"I've come to check up on you," Charlotte said to Rose. "Amy told me that you didn't seem like yourself and asked me to visit." She eyed Cal suspiciously.

"He didn't do anything," Rose assured her friend. "I was a bit upset, but we figured everything out. It's okay. Thanks for checking. Do you want to come in and hang out for a little?"

"Might as well. Could you make some coffee? I didn't have a great night's sleep, and I need more caffeine than usual."

"What's that in your hand?" Rose asked.

"Uh, the coffee I finished five minutes ago, while I was walking here."

Rose lifted an eyebrow then smiled. "You know I love you."

"Yeah, yeah, enough with the mushy stuff."

Charlotte slipped off her shoes and sat down in the living room with Rose. Cal headed to the kitchen, presumably to start the coffee.

A moment later, Charlotte's phone rang.

"Can I get this?" she asked. "It'll only take a minute."

Rose nodded, and Charlotte answered the call.

"No, Mom... No, no, no... No, no... Are you kidding me?... Look, I'm visiting Rose right now. Could we talk about this another time? Or never, that's okay, too... Yes, I was serious about that... Um..." Charlotte lifted the phone away from her ear. "Rose, my mom wants to speak to you."

"Me?"

"Apparently."

Rose accepted the phone. "Hi, Bonnie. How are you?"

Charlotte's mother ignored the pleasantries. "Don't you think Charlotte should get married on the beach in Ashton Corners? I think it would be very nice. I'm watching a new wedding reality show, and there was a ceremony on the beach and it was so lovely. But Charlotte wants to get married in Toronto."

"Considering that most people she knows are in Toronto, it makes sense."

"But I'm in Ashton Corners, and I count for a dozen people because I'm her mother!"

Bonnie was speaking loudly, and even though the phone wasn't on speakerphone, Charlotte could probably hear what was being said. She rolled her eyes and shook her head.

"There's a lack of accommodation in Ashton Corners, though," Rose said, "which is awkward for wedding guests, and the location is inconvenient for people who are flying in."

Bonnie huffed. "At least convince her to let me bake the cake."

"You're volunteering to make the wedding cake? That's a big undertaking."

"You think I can't do it? I've been watching so many baking shows. One is all about wedding cakes—I take notes during it."

"Maybe you could make a special cake for the rehearsal dinner instead?" Rose suggested.

"Hmm. Perhaps you're right. That will give me practice, then I can make Julie's wedding cake! So smart, Rose. Do you think Charlotte would like one of those, what do you call it, hyper-realistic cakes? Shaped like a giant coffee cup?"

"That might be a little ambitious."

They spoke for another minute or two before Rose passed the phone back to Charlotte. As Charlotte ended the call, Rose couldn't help wondering what her own mother would be like if Rose were getting married. The thought of her mother not being there for her wedding caused an ache in Rose's chest. They'd never get to discuss-slash-argue over dresses and seating arrangements, though Rose's mom wouldn't have insisted on being as involved as Charlotte's, especially if she were unwell at the time and her voice had taken on that horrible dullness that it had when she was severely depressed.

Sometimes Rose wondered how different her life would be if her mom had lived. She may never have moved to Toronto. But she tried not to dwell on what hadn't happened.

Cal walked into the room with two mugs of coffee, one for Rose and one for Charlotte.

"You want to join us?" Rose asked him.

"Nah, I'm going out to get something. I'll be back soon."

He gave her a quick kiss, and she couldn't help watching him as he walked away, admiring his broad back and…well, his ass, to be honest.

"I'm happy for you." Charlotte lifted her mug. "Especially since he makes really good coffee, which, as you know, is of critical importance to me."

Charlotte stayed until she finished her coffee, and Rose was tidying the kitchen when Cal returned.

"I got you a present," he said. "Well, a few presents, and they're for both of us."

He took her hand—the feel of her hand in his was no longer a novelty, but it was no less pleasant than before—and led her into the dining room. On the table, there was a tiny cactus and two other plants.

"They're like…" He scratched the back of his neck. "This made more sense in my head. You don't want kids, and we can figure out the pet thing later, but I thought we could have houseplants. They can move to wherever we live and continue to grow the longer we're together. I mean, if I don't accidentally kill them, but I'll try my best… Rose, are you crying?"

"Don't worry, they're happy tears. I like the plants."

She grabbed her phone and took a picture of each plant so

they'd have a record of how big they were at the beginning. Then she took a picture of Shelly and Fred "eating" the plants.

Fred the Alpaca: *Look what our humans got. Nom nom nom. Do you think they'll notice if we eat the cactus?*

Penguin Pip: *Are you sure it's safe for alpacas to eat cacti?*

Fabulous the Unicorn: *A cactus is a FABULOUSLY tasty treat.*

Shelly the Turtle: *Don't worry, Fred. If you get a tummy ache, I'll look after you.*

Merry Lamb: *You guys are so cute.*

Merry Lamb: *Not as cute as me, but still.*

Rose was about to put away her phone, but then she noticed Penguin Pip's latest picture. The penguin stood next to something tastier than a spiky cactus: poutine.

Fred the Alpaca: *Penguin Pip, are you a Canadian penguin?*

Penguin Pip: *I've lived in Montreal ever since I was a wee baby penguin.*

Fred the Alpaca: *Can Shelly and I take a road trip to visit you? We might be nearby in Ottawa later this summer. We can meet at the poutine place!*

Penguin Pip: *OMG I am such a special penguin.*

Feeling like a bit of a weirdo, Rose turned to her boyfriend. She was considering a trip to Montreal to have poutine with a plushie she'd met on the internet—though first, she wanted to know something about Penguin Pip's human—but she wasn't surprised that it didn't bother Cal.

He set aside her phone. "I've been waiting to do something for more than an hour."

He crushed her against his chest and pressed his lips to hers. And as he kissed her, their past—beginning with their first kiss at Nautilus—and future flashed before her.

And then it was hard to think at all because oh my God, the scrape of his beard felt nice against her cheek and his tongue really was incredible. She was eager to remove these silly clothes that were getting in the way of her touching his skin.

Today had been an emotional roller coaster, but in the end, they'd been able to talk rather than breaking up, and she was feeling pretty good about how things stood.

"You want to come home with me?" he asked with a wink. "I have a bed just upstairs."

"I'm sorry for what I said to you," Levi told Cal.

Cal shrugged and took a sip of his beer. "It's okay. You weren't wrong, but it's different when I know she's the right one for me. I'm gonna do everything I can to make sure this works."

He glanced at the time on his phone. He was only staying at the pub for one drink. Rose was having dinner with her friends, and he was meeting them later at the cider bar.

He'd met some of them before. Charlotte, on a couple of occasions. Amy, since she lived next door and was technically his landlord. Sierra, way back when he was looking for a place to live, which wasn't all that long ago, come to think of it. But a lot had changed since then.

"We should go on a double date sometime," Marv said. "I promise not to be too late. I've been putting systems in place so I'm never an hour behind schedule anymore."

"You have to bring her next time we all meet up," Meena said.

"I will." Cal drained his beer and stood. "I gotta bounce. See you later."

It was about a twenty-five-minute walk to Ossington Cider Bar. Even though it was dark, it was still fairly hot, but Cal wasn't complaining. He was used to cutting grass at the hottest time of the day; this was much more pleasant.

He couldn't help whistling as he approached the cider bar. He didn't know shit about cider, but he was gonna see Rose. Although he lived with her and saw her every day, he still grinned at the sight of her, sitting at a large table with several other people.

Hanging out with her friends for the first time was much less terrifying than meeting her dad, and that had gone well, other than when his parents had interrupted. He might not be able to carry on a conversation about Nicole's boyfriend's research—earlier, Rose had provided a quick rundown of everyone who'd be here—but it was gonna be okay. He was with Rose, and he'd do everything in his power to make sure he always would be. Nobody was beautiful and smart and accepting and fun like she was.

Amy was like a unicorn plushie, Rose decided.

Charlotte, on the other hand, was a shark plushie. She had sharp-looking teeth, but she really was squishy and comforting, though Rose supposed that was true of all plushies.

Nicole could be a peacock plushie with fabulous tail feathers, although weren't the male peacocks the ones with the really nice feathers?

Sierra could be a smiling Brussels sprout plushie. Yes, those existed. Rose had checked.

"Hey, babe."

Rose startled as Cal took the seat beside her.

"Or was I not supposed to sit here?" he asked playfully. "There was a purse on the chair. Were you saving it—"

"For you, obviously."

"You seemed surprised to see me."

"I just got distracted, thinking about all my friends as plushies."

He didn't say she was strange. No, he was just grinning at her, like he was so glad to see her no matter what she was thinking. Once again, she couldn't help feeling a little overwhelmed by how lucky she was.

But this wasn't a dream. It was entirely real.

In the weeks since her father's visit, she'd still freaked out a few times. And there had been a day, after a poor night's sleep, when it felt like there was a mountain of bricks sitting on her chest. So, no, life wasn't perfect, but it was pretty damn good, and she believed she and Cal would be together for a long time to come. They'd even had his parents over for lunch last weekend, and while it hadn't been entirely comfortable, it hadn't gone too badly.

What kind of plushie would Cal be? Maybe an enormous Pikachu? Or just a mountain of all the best plushies?

Well, she should probably introduce him to her friends.

"Everyone, this is Cal," she said.

It was the biggest table they'd ever had at Ossington Cider Bar, since there were ten of them here today. Amy and Victor (Hudson was with a babysitter), Charlotte and Mike, Nicole and David, Sierra and Jake…and Rose and Cal. Rose had watched with a little envy as her friends coupled up, but now it was her turn. And she was happy for all of them.

She sipped her blood orange cider then handed it to Cal. "What do you think?"

He tried it. "Mmm. Maybe I'll order one of these."

"I recommend the passionfruit peach cider," Nicole said. "It's nice and sweet."

Charlotte made a face and held up her glass. "This one's dry, like a cider should be."

Cal frowned. "How can a liquid be dry?"

"It means it's not too sweet," Rose said.

"Well, I'll get the blood orange one. It was tasty."

"Before I forget," Charlotte said. "I'm going wedding dress shopping in two weeks. Does anyone want to come with me? Fair warning: my mother and Julie will be there."

"Hey!" Julie said as she walked by.

"You know I want to go," Nicole said.

"Me, too," Amy said.

"On the Saturday?" Sierra put a finger to her lips. "I have to work that day."

"Rose?" Charlotte turned to her.

"I'm not sure." Rose thought this shopping trip sounded rather stressful.

"That's okay. You don't need to come—there will be more than enough opinions—but at a later date, you'll have to try on bridesmaids' dresses."

"Why…oh! Of course I'll be your bridesmaid, Charlotte." Rose gave her a hug.

"You all get to be bridesmaids," Charlotte said. "Don't worry, nobody's left out, unless you try to force-feed me pizza with pineapple."

"Wouldn't dream of it," Nicole said.

"Or come between me and my coffee."

"We all know that's just asking for trouble, don't worry."

The conversation made Rose a little sentimental. She'd met most of these women at university, when they were barely adults, and now…

"Hey," Cal said to her, leaning close. "You okay?"

"Yeah." She smiled at him. "Just thinking."

"Good things about me, I hope."

"Obviously."

So much had changed since Rose had met Charlotte, Sierra, and Nicole, but they were still friends. And Rose had someone new in her life, too, whom she believed would also be with her through all the rough patches.

"I have special plans for you tomorrow," she told Cal, poking his chest.

"Yeah? What are these special plans?"

"You'll just have to wait and see."

∿

Rose had once seen the contestants on a baking show make pretzels, and for some reason, she'd wanted to try it ever since. Earlier, she'd grilled hot dogs and set out a few bottles of Cal's favorite beer, and now she was serving him homemade pretzels with cheese dip as he watched a baseball game.

This wasn't exactly her ideal Sunday afternoon, but he'd planned that perfect day for her, and she wanted to do something special for him.

And in a way, it was pretty perfect.

Because she was with Cal.

"Wow, I can't believe you made these," he said.

"And I did it without mixing up Celsius and Fahrenheit," she teased.

He laughed as he picked up a pretzel from the platter she'd set on the coffee table. Then he took a big bite. "They're great. Thanks."

She was about to return to the kitchen to clean up, but when he tugged her onto the couch with him, she figured that could wait a few minutes.

She lay with her head in his lap, and she grabbed the kraken to squeeze as he stroked her hair. Watching baseball had truly never been more fun. Cal muttered something about what was happening on-screen, but she didn't catch it. She helped herself to a pretzel and tore off a small piece.

Right now, she felt peaceful. Content. But at some point, her brain would be less cooperative, and it was just something she had to live with. Unlike her mother, she accepted that she struggled with mental illness, and her illness wasn't her fault. Well, sometimes she still had a little trouble believing the latter, but she did her best.

Mom, I wish you hadn't blamed yourself. Or me.

And I really do wish you could have met Cal.

She squeezed her kraken tight, and Cal planted a kiss on the top of her head. She didn't want to distract him too much from the game, but she raised herself up so she could give him a quick kiss on his lips.

Then she grabbed another pretzel and got up to water their plants.

EPILOGUE

A few years later...

It was the end of an era.

Rose stood on the sidewalk and looked at the semi-detached Victorian that had been her home. The house was the reason she'd met Amy, who came to stand beside her now. There was a baby in her arms, and Hudson was affixed to her leg.

"I remember the day I moved in," Amy said. "I was so excited to start my new life in Toronto. I never imagined I'd end up getting married to the hot guy next door who was cutting the grass shirtless that day."

Rose chuckled. She and Cal were moving to their new home today, and Amy had sold the house she'd inherited.

So much had happened since Cal had first become Rose's roommate.

Charlotte and Mike had gotten married—in Toronto, not Ashton Corners, and a professionally baked cake had been served at the reception. They had a daughter, now eighteen months old, who showed, as Charlotte lovingly put it, a disturbing fondness for pineapple in all forms, particularly on pizza. Her favorite toy, much to Mike's distress, was a stuffed spider.

Nicole and David had gotten married at City Hall, and they also had a toddler. They'd bought a small house near the building where they used to live in neighboring units.

Sierra and Jake were engaged, and they'd been happily living together ever since Sierra had moved out of the house in the Annex. Sierra's ex-boyfriend, Colton Sanders, was in prison, although his sentence was almost over.

"Hey," Sierra said, walking over to Amy and Rose. "The moving truck isn't here yet?"

"Nope. Any minute," Rose said.

Cal walked out of the house with two large bags of plushies, and she smiled. The plushies and plants—all of which were healthy—would be going to the new house in his car, rather than the moving truck.

After putting the bags in the back seat, Cal came to stand behind Rose and pulled her into his arms. She squeezed his hands and relaxed against him.

Their new house had three bedrooms: one for each of them and one guest room. She still wasn't the greatest at sharing a bed, but that was okay. Relationships weren't always what you imagined they'd be. They were weird and wonderful and amazing.

Every day, he told her how much he loved her.

Every day, he made her feel special.

Yes, Cal Dempsey, with those big arms that were wrapped snugly around her, was one of the best things that had ever happened to her, no doubt about it. Discovering that Penguin Pip was owned by a pretty cool female scientist a few years older than Rose? Also good, but not quite as wonderful.

Rose and Cal had been married for almost a year now. Their simple wedding last spring had been planned to cause her as little stress as possible, and she'd loved every minute of it. The food?

Delicious. Cal in a tux? *Mmm.* She'd worn a lacy white dress that had made her look stunning, and it had rendered him speechless.

Although her mental health hadn't been perfect in the past few years, she'd felt supported through all of it, and she'd improved her coping skills.

"Truck!" Hudson said, pointing. "It's here!"

"You ready?" Cal whispered, his breath and his beard tickling Rose's ear.

"Yep. Let's do this."

She tried to walk, but he held her firm in his arms. He turned her around and pressed a kiss to her mouth.

"Sorry," he said. "I couldn't help it."

"You're not sorry," she said.

He grinned. "No, I'm not. Just like I'm not sorry I decided to live here. With you."

He released her, but she stood on her toes to kiss him again. She was very much in love with her husband and always would be.

That night, when she entered her new bedroom, she found Fred the Alpaca and Shelly the Turtle on her pillow, next to a brand-new cactus plushie.

Cal was the sweetest roommate ever, no doubt about it.

ACKNOWLEDGMENTS

Thank you to my editor, Latoya C. Smith, for helping me improve this book and catching all my errors, and to Flirtation Designs for the cover.

Thank you also to Toronto Romance Writers, plus my family, for all your support.

And to my readers, who have made this career possible for me. Thank you for reading the Cider Bar Sisters books!

ABOUT THE AUTHOR

Jackie Lau decided she wanted to be a writer when she was in grade two, sometime between writing "The Heart That Got Lost" and "The Land of Shapes." She later studied engineering and worked as a geophysicist before turning to writing romance novels. Jackie lives in Toronto with her husband, and despite living in Canada her whole life, she hates winter. When she's not writing, she enjoys gelato, gourmet donuts, cooking, hiking, and reading on the balcony when it's raining.

To learn more and sign up for her newsletter,
visit jackielaubooks.com.

Baldwin Village Series

One Bed for Christmas (prequel novella)

The Ultimate Pi Day Party

Ice Cream Lover

Man vs. Durian

Chin-Williams Series

Not Another Family Wedding

He's Not My Boyfriend

www.ingramcontent.com/pod-product-compliance
Lightning Source LLC
Chambersburg PA
CBHW030820210726
48290CB00002B/687